镜子书·新编经典童话绘本系列

友爱篇

THE SNOW QUEEN

冰雪女王

[意] 曼纽拉·阿德雷亚尼 绘 [丹] 安徒生 著 李静滢 译

SPM 南方传媒 | 广东人民出版社

·广州·

绘者 曼纽拉·阿德雷亚尼

意大利插画师、平面设计师。先后从事平面设计、动画创作、插画绘制工作。

曾获欧洲设计学院（都灵分院）动画专业博士生奖学金。在Làstrego & Testa工作室工作期间，设计制作了《阿拉丁历险记》等一系列动画片，并在意大利国家电视台播放。

2011年起，与基准出版社、学乐印度公司合作，开始了自由插画家的职业生涯。先后创作了《木偶奇遇记》《爱丽丝漫游奇境》《绿野仙踪》《白雪公主》《小王子》和《美女与野兽》等绘本。其绘本作品曾获世界三大绘本大奖之一的“凯特·格林纳威奖”提名。

做个友爱的孩子

在一个可爱的小镇上，住着小女孩格尔达和小男孩加伊。他们是一对好伙伴，每天一起玩耍，亲密无间。

可是有一天，一块魔鬼的镜子碎片落到了加伊眼睛里，从此以后他再也感受不到友情的温暖和快乐了。

不久，加伊被掌控着寒冷的冰雪女王带走，格尔达为了寻找自己的伙伴，开始了漫长的旅程。最后，格尔达用友爱之心融化了加伊眼睛里的冰冷碎片，让他重新感受到世界的美好。

请注意！现在我们要讲一个很吓人、很吓人的故事。

故事的开头是这样的：世界上最最邪恶的大魔头，也就是魔鬼，有一天干成了一件大坏事，这让他喜不自禁。这是怎么回事呢？原来呀，魔鬼运用他掌握的法术，制造了一面神奇的镜子。这面镜子会把一切美好的东西都隐藏起来，只呈现出与原来面貌不一样的可怕镜像。一切丑陋的东西用这镜子一照，都只会更加丑陋；再漂亮的风景用这镜子一照，都会变成煮烂了的菠菜。最漂亮的人用这面镜子一照，不是脸被拉扯得像一张铺在平底锅上的大饼，就是面孔扭曲得完全辨认不出来。最微小的瑕疵都会被这面镜子无限放大，比如说，要是谁的脸上有个小雀斑，那它在镜子中肯定可以扩大到铺满整张脸的程度。魔鬼觉得这真是太有趣了。要知道，即使一个人心中有美好的想法，在这镜子里也只会变成邪恶的念头，因此魔鬼对自己这奇妙的发明感到无比满意。

那些进魔鬼学校学巫术的巫师全都说自己见证了奇迹，因为他们终于从这面魔镜中看到了世界和人类的“本来面目”。那些巫师一起带着魔镜四处游逛，到了最后，没有一个国家不曾被这面镜子照到过，没有一个人不曾被这面镜子歪曲过。可是他们并没有因此满足，反而想做更多的坏事，最后他们决定飞到天上去把天使戏弄一番。他们带着镜子飞向天堂。一想到即将惹出的乱子，他们就忍不住恣意狂笑，笑得连镜子都拿不稳了。眼看他们就要飞到天使聚集的天堂，可是镜子伴着他们的怪笑不停颤抖，最后从他们手中滑落到了地面，摔成了不计其数的碎片。

这样一来，镜子造成的祸害就更大了，因为镜子的有些碎片比沙粒还要细小，它们被春天的大风吹到了世界各地，只要飞进人的眼睛里就会贴在那儿不动。眼里进了镜子碎片的人要么看什么都是扭曲的，要么只能看到事物坏的一面，因为每块小小的碎片都具有整面镜子的魔力。有的镜子碎片甚至能钻进人的心里。结果当然非常可怕：这颗心会变得像冰块一样冷。

镜子的部分碎片很大，一些不知情的玻璃商把它们做成了窗户玻璃。人们透过这样的玻璃去看窗外，看到的是可怕的、残酷的世界，外面居住着庞大的怪物，因此他们就再也不敢出门了。有些碎片被做成了眼镜，这就太糟糕了，因为人们戴眼镜本来是为了更清晰更好地看东西，可是透过这样的眼镜看东西，结果当然适得其反。这一切让魔鬼兴奋得手舞足蹈，把肚子都笑疼了，而镜子的碎片依然在空中乱飞。

我们要讲的故事就是这样开始的。接下来会发生什么呢？

在一座大城市里，居民非常多，房子特别拥挤，连盖个小花园的地方都没有，大多数人只好在花盆里种几朵小花。我们故事的主人公就是住在这座城市里的两个穷孩子，他们运用自己的想象力，为自己创造出了比花盆略微大一点的小花园。

两个孩子的家离得很近，两家阁楼的屋顶差不多挨在了一起，屋檐下有道集水沟。每家的阁楼都开着扇小窗，可以从这扇窗钻到那扇窗里去。两家的父母分别在窗外放了两个大木头箱子，箱子里分别种了一小棵玫瑰和烹饪所需的香料植物。两棵玫瑰都长得枝繁叶茂。

有一天，这两对父母把各家的木头箱横放在集水沟上，箱子两端靠着两家的窗户，就好像开满花的堤岸。豌豆藤从箱子上垂下来，玫瑰伸展出长长的枝条。它们在窗子上盘绕着，构成了绿叶和花朵织成的凯旋门。两个大箱子都很高，所以两家父母允许两个孩子从窗户爬出去，一起坐在玫瑰花下的小凳子上，在那里愉快地玩耍。整个春天和夏天，他们都是这样开心地度过的。到了冬天，玫瑰花丛的叶子落光了，窗户冻住了，玻璃上结满了冰。他们就把一个铜板弄热，轮流把热铜板贴在窗玻璃上，融出一个小小的、圆圆的窥视孔。于是两扇窗的窥视孔后面都会有一只明亮的眼睛在向外张望，眼睛的主人当然就是这两个孩子。他们不是兄妹，却亲如兄妹，一天也不愿意分开。

男孩的名字叫加伊，女孩的名字叫格尔达。

夏天，两个孩子只需从阁楼的窗户轻轻一跃，就能在一起；在冬天，他们要走出房子，爬下一大段阶梯，然后再爬上一大段阶梯，才能在一起。即使是在风雪交加的日子里，两个孩子仍然会相见。

在一个雪天，老祖母对他们说：“在空中飞舞的不是雪花，而是成群的白色蜜蜂！”

“它们也有蜂后吗？”小男孩问。他知道每个蜜蜂群中都有一个蜂后。

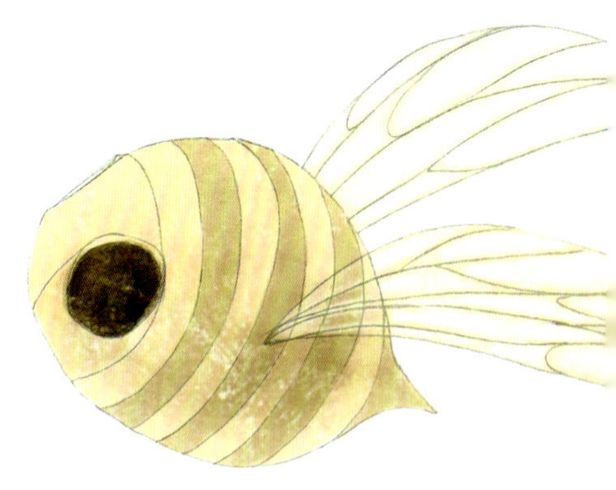

“当然有！”祖母说，“她就在白色蜜蜂最密集的地方，她比其他白色蜜蜂的体型都大。她从来不会落到地面，每次要贴近地面时，她就又会飞得高高的，回到幽暗的天空中。她常常在冬天的夜晚飞过城市的街道，朝窗户里张望，然后窗户上就会结出形状奇特的冰花，好像开着花朵似的。”

听到这里，两个孩子齐声说道：“是的，我见到过冰花！”

于是他们相信祖母说的是真的。

“冰雪王后能飞进我们屋子里来吗？”小女孩子问。

“欢迎她飞进来，”男孩子说，“我要把她安置在温暖的炉子上，那样她就会融化了。”

老祖母慈爱地抚摸着他们的头发，转换了话题，又开始讲别的故事。

一天晚上，小加伊已经脱了一半衣服，却又好奇地爬到窗户旁的椅子上去，从那个小窥视孔往外张望。

他看到两朵大大的雪花朝他徐徐落下来，其中更大的一朵落到了花箱子的一角。

这朵雪花越长越大，最后变成了一个高挑的女子，她披着纤薄的白纱，那白纱仿佛由风中旋转的雪花编织而成。她非常美丽，非常优雅，然而构成她身体的，却是晶莹的、亮闪闪的冰。她是有生命的，她直视着前方，但是眼神里并没有和平与安宁。她对加伊点了点头，慢慢地招了招手。加伊害怕起来，跳下椅子，此时窗外刮起了一阵旋风，那个冰人变成了一只白色的大鸟，拍动翅膀飞走了。

加伊在第二天早上醒来时发现，街道上的所有房子一夜之间都覆盖上了厚厚的一层冰。不过在那之后，一切都与往年一样，寒冰渐渐消融，春天到来了。太阳暖暖地照耀着，草木冒出了绿芽，燕子筑起巢。窗户打开了，加伊和格尔达又开始在他们的小花园里相会。这年夏天，玫瑰花开得格外美丽，两个孩子手拉着手，在温煦的阳光下欣赏夜里长出来的漂亮花蕾。这些瑰丽的玫瑰花就好像永远都开不尽似的。在如此美好的夏日来到室外，来到玫瑰花旁，是多么幸福啊！

有一天下午，加伊和格尔达坐在一起读一本绘有动物的画册。大教堂尖塔上的钟敲了五下，这时加伊突然喊了起来："啊！我觉得心刺痛了一下！还有东西落到我的眼睛里了！"小女孩格尔达捧起他的脸，想帮他把落进眼里的东西弄出来。加伊眨着眼睛，但是格尔达没发现他眼睛里有什么东西。

"应该已经出来了！"格尔达说。

但她说错了，发生的事情非常严重。

落到加伊眼里的正是魔鬼镜子的一小片玻璃屑。你应该还记得，那是一面可怕的魔镜，

会把一切伟大和善良的东西都照得藐小和可憎，

把所有罪恶、肮脏的东西全都放大到格外显眼。

可怜的小加伊啊！魔镜的碎片不仅落进了他的眼睛，还落进了他的心。他的心很快就变得像冰块一样了！

小加伊感受到的痛楚很快就消失了，但碎片还藏在身体里。

“你为什么要哭呢？”他问格尔达，接着就无缘无故地发起了脾气。“你哭的样子太丑了！别哭了，我什么事都没有！”然后他忽然嚷了起来：“啊呸！那朵玫瑰花被虫子咬了一口！你看，那一朵也长歪了！哎呀，这些玫瑰全都丑死了！比种它们的木头箱子还难看！”说完，他狠狠踢了种花的箱子一脚，又用力扯下了两朵玫瑰花。

“怎么了，加伊，你在干什么啊？”格尔达惊叫起来，但是加伊看到她惊惶的样子，马上又揪下了一朵玫瑰，然后从窗户跳回自己家，不再理睬善良的格尔达。

晚些时候，格尔达带了本画册到加伊家里找他，他却刻薄地说这本书只配给小孩子看。晚饭后，祖母像往常一样给他们讲童话故事，加伊却不断插嘴说“那又怎么样”。他还跟在祖母后面，抢她的眼镜，模仿她的样子讲话。他模仿得惟妙惟肖。后来他在大街上也模仿起祖母的样子，看到他的人都会被他逗得哈哈大笑。很快他就开始模仿邻居，模仿别人身上古怪和丑恶的特点。他太善于模仿了，大家都说：“这孩子可真机灵啊！”然而实际上，这都要归因于落进他眼里和心里的魔镜碎片。他之所以会这样做，之所以会讥笑小格尔达，也都是因为魔镜的碎片在作祟。那年的冬天到来后，加伊的游戏与往年完全不同。

有一天，雪下得很大，他拿着一面放大镜走出来，提起他的蓝色上衣的下摆，让雪花落到它上面。“格尔达，你来用这面放大镜看看雪花吧！”他说。在放大镜下，每一片雪花都被放大了，看起来就像一朵朵美丽的花儿，或是有多个尖角的星星。“你看，多漂亮啊！真是完美！”加伊说，“雪花多有趣呀，不像那些傻透了的玫瑰。你看到了吗，这些雪花是完美的，它们整齐划一，只要不融化……”不过，还没等格尔达回答，他就转身走回家里，再出来时戴上了厚手套，还背着一个小雪橇。

“加伊，你要去哪儿呀？”格尔达在他身后喊道。

“去中心广场，很多小孩都在那里玩雪。”加伊边回答边在路口拐了个弯。

在广场上，那些最大胆的孩子经常会把雪橇偷偷拴在大人的马车后边，让马车带着他们跑好长一段路。他们觉得这非常好玩。他们玩得正开心时，一架漆成雪白色的大雪橇滑了过来，上面坐着一个人，那人身穿柔软的白色皮袄，头戴厚厚的白色毛帽子。大雪橇绕着广场滑了两圈，然后停在广场中央。

加伊悄悄溜过去，把自己的小雪橇用绳子系到白色的大雪橇上，准备跟着它一起滑行。他刚打好最后一个结，大雪橇就滑了起来，仿佛有人下了命令一般。大雪橇越滑越快，迅速穿过大街小巷，毫不停留。娴熟地操纵着大雪橇的那个人扭过头，友好地对加伊点了点头，就好像两人早已相识。加伊每次想解开自己的小雪橇的绳子，那人都会对他点点头，加伊解不开绳子，只好尽量坐稳，免得从雪橇上摔下去。雪橇以惊人的速度往前滑，很快就滑出了城门。这时开始下大雪了，茫茫雪雾中伸手不见五指，然而雪橇还在向前滑。加伊又一次尝试着解开绳子，却还是解不开，绳子已经彻底冻住了。他大声尖叫，但是没人理他。大雪纷飞，雪橇飞一般疾驰。有时雪橇会颠起来，那或许是滑过了篱笆和沟渠。加伊吓得要命。他想祷告，却想不起祷告词，头脑里出现的只有乘法表。

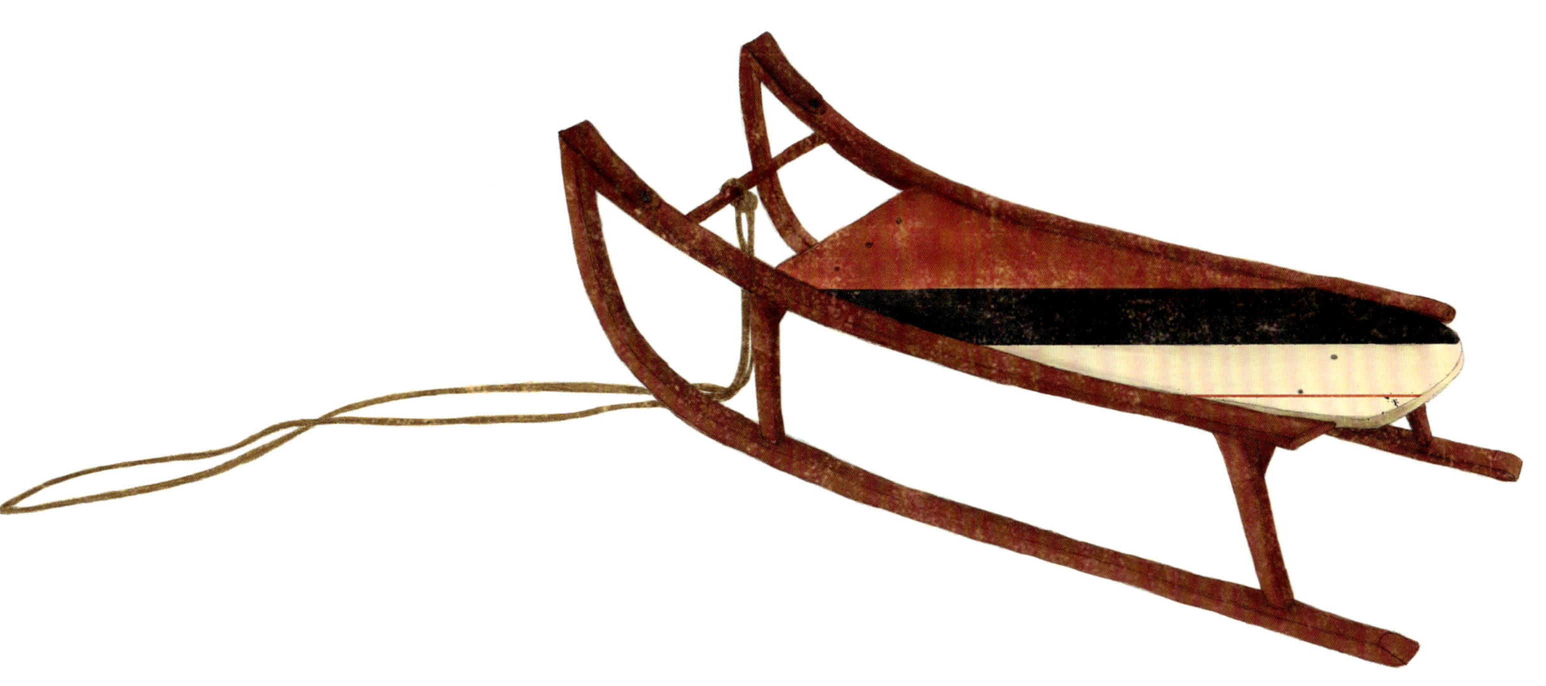

雪下得更大了，最后雪花看起来宛如巨大的白鸟。那架大雪橇突然向旁边一跳，停了下来，滑雪橇的人站起身，摘下帽子，露出了面孔，是个女子。加伊首先注意到她的皮衣和帽子其实是用雪做的，然后加伊抬起头，认出了她的模样。她长得又高又苗条，全身上下闪烁着白光。她就是冰雪女王。

“我们的雪橇滑得真棒，”她带着冷冰冰的微笑对加伊说道，“不过这么冷的天气，你肯定要冻坏了，钻进我的皮衣里来暖和一下吧。”她继续微笑着，拉起加伊的手，让他坐进她的雪橇，就坐在她的身旁。她用自己的雪花皮衣把加伊包裹好，加伊感觉自己坠入了雪山之中。“你还冷吗？”她问道，接着就亲吻了一下加伊的前额。这一吻啊，比寒冰还要冷！这冷冽的一吻，直逼加伊已经结了冰的心脏，让他感到自己马上就要死了。不过这感觉转瞬即逝，然后他就不觉得难受了，也不再怕冷了，尽管前一刻他还冻得直打哆嗦。“小雪橇！别忘了我的小雪橇！”加伊说道。但是冰雪女王又吻了一下加伊，忽然间他就完全忘记了小格尔达和家里所有的人。“我不能再亲你了，”她大笑着说，“再亲下去你会死掉的。”

加伊凝视着她。她太美了！他想象不出比她更迷人更聪慧的面孔。与从前她在窗外对他招手时不一样，她现在看上去不像是由冰块构成的了。在加伊眼里，她是完美无瑕的，他一点也不觉得害怕了。加伊此时感到非常轻松自在。他告诉冰雪女王，他擅长心算，连小数都算得出来；他知道很多国家的面积和人口。冰雪女王一边听一边对他微笑着。这时加伊才觉得自己知道的东西太少了，他把自己的这个想法也告诉了冰雪女王，问她能不能教给自己一些新的知识。她点了点头，然后仰起头，一言未发，一个手势未做，雪橇就突然飞上了天空。暴风雪在呼啸怒号，他们在轻快地飞行。他们飞过树林，飞过湖泊，飞过花园和村庄。在他们下方，寒风在呼啸，豺狼在嗥叫，雪花在飘舞。在他们头上飞着一群哇哇乱叫的黑乌鸦，一轮大大的明月挂在空中，月光照彻长长的冬夜。

天亮时，加伊在冰雪女王脚边睡着了。

加伊彻夜未归，小格尔达的心情可想而知。

他到底去哪儿了呢？格尔达毫无头绪，她问遍了城里的人，但是谁也不知道加伊的去向。那天与加伊一起在斜坡上玩耍的一些男孩子只记得有一架漂亮的大雪橇停在广场上，他们看到加伊把他的小雪橇系到了大雪橇上，和大雪橇一起滑出了城门，但他们对此也并不十分确定。他们对此的记忆如同蒙上了一层浓雾，变得模糊混沌。他们唯一能清晰地记得的就是，当时气温骤降，他们回家时感觉都快冻僵了。

总而言之，谁也不知道加伊去了哪里，不知道他是和谁一起离开的。

后来，大家都说，加伊肯定是掉进流过城边的那条河里淹死了。许多人为加伊落下了眼泪，小格尔达更是哭得心都要碎了。

那是小女孩格尔达度过的最漫长最忧伤的冬季。尽管如此，春天还是与温煦的太阳一起到来了！

格尔达来到她与加伊曾经共度美好时光的花园，看着那些含苞待放的玫瑰，然后抬头看着春天的太阳，突然对太阳说："加伊淹死了！"

"不，我不相信！"太阳坚定地回答。

"我告诉你，加伊死了，消失了！"她对飞过的燕子说。

"我们不相信！"燕子回答。

到了最后，格尔达自己也不相信加伊已经死了。

一天早晨，她下定了决心，说道："我要穿上那双新的红鞋子，那双加伊没见过的新鞋子。我要去河边寻找他！"她说做就做，毫不迟疑。

老祖母还在睡觉，格尔达不想叫醒祖母，只是轻轻亲吻了祖母的额头，对她说了声再见，然后就穿上红鞋子，独自走出城外，去河边寻找朋友的下落。

“是你把加伊带走了吗？”她对河水说，“如果你能让他回家，我就把这双鞋送给你！”她觉得波浪似乎在对她示意，于是她脱下她最心爱的红鞋子，把鞋子抛进河里，可是波浪立刻又把它们推回到岸上。

这条河似乎不愿意接受格尔达最心爱的红鞋子，这或许是因为它无法把加伊还给她。不过格尔达认为是鞋子抛得不够远，因此她爬上了停在芦苇中的一条船，走到船头，用力把这双鞋抛到河里。但是这条船没系牢，她在上面一走动，船就离开了停泊的地方，从岸边慢慢漂走了。格尔达发现船在动，想赶快下船，但是还没等她从船上跳下去，船就已经离岸边很远了，而且在波浪的推动下漂得越来越快。小格尔达害怕地哭了起来，可是听到她哭声的只有麻雀。麻雀无法把她送回到陆地，于是它们跟着船一起飞，一边飞一边唱着歌，好像在说：“我们在这儿呀！我们在这儿呀！”

船顺流而下，小格尔达光着脚坐在船上，她的红鞋子跟在船后面漂浮着，但是漂不到船边来，因为鞋子跟不上船的速度。河两岸风光秀丽，古树成荫，还点缀着漂亮的花朵，只是一个人也看不到。

“或许这条河会送我去见加伊吧。”格尔达这样一想，就又觉得开心了。她不再害怕，而是坐着欣赏岸上的田园风光。

船漂呀漂呀，她看到了一片漂亮的樱桃园，里面有一座农舍。农舍的窗户是红色、蓝色和黄色的，屋顶是茅草做的。

这时河水把船推向岸边，于是格尔达用力挥着手，大声喊起来，直到一位上了年纪的老太太拄着拐杖走出农舍。她头上戴着一顶大草帽，上面装饰着花朵。“可怜的小姑娘啊！”老太太对格尔达说，“你怎么会跑到这波涛滚滚的河上，漂到离城市这么远的地方呢？”说着，她走下河岸，用拐杖把船钩住后拖到岸边，帮小格尔达下了船。

格尔达终于又回到了岸上。她很高兴，但是也有些害怕这位陌生人。

“孩子，讲一讲你是怎么来到这儿的吧。”老太太说。

格尔达把前因后果全都给她讲了一遍，她边听边摇头，嘴里念叨着“嗯哼嗯哼”。格尔达把一切都讲完后，问她有没有见过加伊，老太太回答说，他肯定会往这边来的。她叫格尔达不要太难过，就安安心心地待在这房子里，尝尝樱桃赏赏花，画册上再美的花朵也不如她种的花儿漂亮，因为她的花儿个个都能讲故事。

说完这些，老太太牵着格尔达的手，领她走进农舍小屋，随手锁上了门。

小屋的窗户开得很高，玻璃是红色、蓝色和黄色的，透过这些玻璃照进来的阳光也变成了彩色的。桌上放着些诱人的红樱桃。格尔达饿坏了，吃了两大捧樱桃。她不再感到害怕了。

老太太用一把金梳子替格尔达梳头发，让她漂亮的金色卷发更好地衬托出她美丽的圆圆的脸。

“我一直希望能有个像你这样可爱的小女孩，”她说，“你会看到，我们两个将会多么幸福地生活在一起！”老太太梳着格尔达的头发时，格尔达渐渐忘记了加伊。原来老太太是个女巫，但她不是个坏女巫。她的咒语不害人，她只是太孤独了，所以想让小格尔达留下来陪着她。

她看到格尔达的心情已经放松下来，就走进了花园，用拐杖指着所有盛开着的玫瑰花，让它们都沉到了黑色的泥土中，谁也看不出它们曾经存在过。女巫担心的是，如果格尔达看见了玫瑰花，就会想起自己家的玫瑰花，就会想起加伊，然后就会离开她。园中的玫瑰花全都消失后，女巫把格尔达领进花园。

格尔达一走出屋子就瞪大了眼睛。这个花园多么芬芳，多么漂亮啊！所有你能想象到的花儿，这里全都有，而且全都在盛开。格尔达心想，老奶奶说得真对，再美的画册也不如这里的花儿多姿多彩。她欢欣雀跃，一直玩到太阳在大樱桃树后面落下去才恋恋不舍地回农舍。女巫给她准备好了一间卧室，里面有一张漂亮的小床，床上铺着粉色丝绸被，被子上还绣着蓝色的紫罗兰。格尔达睡得很香，做的梦很美好，即使新婚当日的皇后都未必会有这样的好梦。第二天早上，格尔达醒来后又跑到温暖的阳光下与花儿一起玩耍。时间就这样一天又一天地过去。几个月后，格尔达已经认识了每一种花，但是她每次走进花园时总会不由自主地停下来，困惑地盯着一处空空的大花坛看。她当然不知道花坛里曾经种满了玫瑰花，只是觉得那里少了点儿什么。

有一天她突然意识到自己正看着老太太的旧草帽，那上面绘满了五颜六色的花朵，其中最美丽的是一朵玫瑰花。原来，女巫把所有玫瑰花匆匆藏到地底下时，忘记了自己的帽子上还画着这样一朵玫瑰花。想要面面俱到真的是太难了！“这怎么可能呢？”格尔达脱口而出，“花园里怎么会一朵玫瑰花都没有呢？”她跳到花坛中间，找了又找，但是一朵玫瑰也找不到。于是她坐在地上，失落地哭了起来。她的眼泪恰好落到了玫瑰花沉入土中的地方。泪水渗进了土里，润湿了土壤，一株玫瑰立刻从土里冒了出来，枝条上还开着茂盛的花，与当初坠入土里时一模一样。格尔达抱着这株玫瑰，凝视着枝条上的玫瑰花，突然就想起了家中种在箱子里的花，同时也想起了加伊。

“天啊，我已经耽搁了这么久！”小姑娘自言自语道。“我必须去找加伊！你们知道他在什么地方吗？”她问那些玫瑰花，“你们认为他死了吗？”“不，他没有死！”玫瑰花回答，“我们很确定！”“谢谢你们！但我要去哪里找他呢？”格尔达问遍了花园里的所有花朵，却没有得到任何答案。

每朵花都在阳光下做着它们自己的梦，梦的内容都是大地或微风讲给它们听的童话或故事。

第一个开口的是红百合，它说道：“你听到了敲鼓声吗？咚咚！咚咚！总是同样的两个鼓点，咚咚！咚咚！你能听到女人的哀歌吗？那心中的火苗会在火葬堆上的火焰里死去吗？”“你说的话我一点都不懂！”小格尔达诚实地说。“这是我的故事啊！”红百合生气地回答。

“牵牛花要说些什么呢？”“在一条逼仄的山路尽头，有一座古老的城堡。在城堡古老的红墙上，长满了密密的常春藤，叶子一片接一片环绕着阳台，阳台上站着一位美丽的姑娘。姑娘在栏杆前弯下腰，眺望着大路。没有哪朵玫瑰花能比她的容颜更娇美，没有哪朵被风吹落的苹果花能比她更轻盈。你听，她那优雅的丝绸长裙在沙沙作响！但他还没有来！”牵牛花悲伤地讲道。

“你是说加伊还没有来吗？”小格尔达问，“报春花有什么要讲的呢？”

“从树枝上垂下来两根绳子，上面拴着一块长木板。这是个秋千。两个漂亮的小姑娘正在荡秋千，她们穿着雪一样白的衣服，头上系着长长的绿丝带。她们的哥哥站在秋千上，用手臂挽住了绳子。他一只手托着个小碗，另一只手拿着根稻草秆，在吹肥皂泡。秋千飞了起来，五光十色的美丽的肥皂泡飞到了空中。挂在稻草秆上的最后一个肥皂泡也被风吹起来，飘到了空中。秋千继续摇荡。一只像肥皂泡一样轻飘飘的小黑狗用后腿站了起来，也想爬到秋千上。秋千继续摇荡，小黑狗摔了下来，气恼地汪汪叫着。肥皂泡破了，它很失望。一块飞舞的秋千板，一个破灭的肥皂泡，这就是我的歌！”

“你的故事好像很唯美，但你讲得太凄惨了，而且你没提到小加伊。风信子有什么要讲的呢？”

“从前有三姐妹，她们非常漂亮，白皙柔弱。老大穿着红衣服，老二穿着蓝衣服，老三穿着白衣服。她们在月光下，在宁静的小湖边，手挽着手跳舞。她们不是山妖，而是人间的女儿。空气中传来十分甜蜜的馨香，三位姑娘消失在树林里，萤火虫在四周飞来飞去，就像一盏盏小灯笼。”

“你说得我特别难过，”小格尔达说，“你身上的香气这么馥郁，我……”

“叮叮当！叮叮当！”风信子的风铃声打断了格尔达，“我们的铃声并非为加伊而鸣。我们根本都不认识他！我们只是唱着自己的歌，唱着我们唯一知晓的歌。”

格尔达接着走向在翠绿的花叶间微笑的金凤花。“你就像个小太阳，”格尔达说，“如果你知道我在哪里能找到我的玩伴，请你告诉我。”

金凤花发着灿烂的金光，看着格尔达。金凤花会唱一支什么歌呢？它的歌里也没有提到小加伊。“春季到来的第一天，太阳暖洋洋地照进了一个小院子。阳光落在邻居家屋子的白墙上，墙根开出了这个春天的第一朵黄花，

它发着金子般金灿灿的光。老祖母坐在屋外的椅子上，她的小孙女回家看望她。小孙女是个贫穷却美丽的小姑娘，一到家就给了祖母一个吻，这充满爱的吻里藏着金子，那是属于心灵的纯金。金灿灿的光落在嘴唇上，金灿灿的光闪烁在心底，金灿灿的光照亮了整个早晨。这就是我小小的故事！”金凤花说。

“这故事说的是我可怜的老祖母啊！”格尔达叹了口气，说道，“她肯定在想念我，加伊的失踪让我这么难过，祖母找不见我，肯定也是一样的难过。不过我很快就会回家的，我会带着加伊一起回家。问这些花儿一点用都没有，它们只知道唱自己的歌。”说完她把衣服扎起来，好能跑得更快一些。

可是她跨过水仙花时，水仙花绊住了她的脚。格尔达停下来看着黄色水仙花长长的茎，问道：“也许你会知道一点点关于加伊的消息吧？”

水仙花讲了些什么呢？它攀上了格尔达的肩膀，说道：“我能看见我自己！我能看见我自己！在那小小的阁楼里站着位半裸的小小舞蹈家，她一会儿单腿着地，一会儿双腿着地。她踢出腿时整个世界都为之倾倒，但那不过是个幻象。她把水从茶壶里倒出来，倒在手里抓着的织物上，那是她的紧身胸衣。钩子上挂着的那件白色连衣裙也是用壶里的水洗过，在屋顶晒干的。她穿上这件连衣裙，在脖子上围了一条橘黄色的小头巾，把裙子衬得更白了。你看，她用一条腿站着，另一条腿向空中抬起，她的样子多美啊！我能看见我自己！我能看见我自己！”

“你说的这些东西，我一丁点儿都不感兴趣！”格尔达激动地嚷道，“你不应该和我讲这些！”说完，她朝花园的篱笆墙跑去。门是关着的，她拔出生了锈的插销，打开花园的门，光着脚跑到街上。

她扭头往回看了三次，没发现有人出来追她。最后她累得跑不动了，就在一块大石头上坐下来，打量着四周。这时她才发现夏天已经过去了，现在是晚秋时节。在那个美丽的花园里，她没有注意到时间的流逝，因为那里永远是阳光普照，四季鲜花不断。小格尔达叫了出来："啊！我耽搁得太久了！已经是秋天了！我不能再休息了！"于是她起身继续向前走。她的脚走得又酸又痛，周围一片凄冷的景象。柳树细长的叶子已经变黄了，上面结着白霜，树叶一片片掉落下来。李子树上依然挂着果实，但是那些李子太涩了，咬一口就会觉得牙疼。唉！这个世界是多么灰暗，多么凄凉啊！

不知走了多久，格尔达走不动了，只能再一次停下来休息。一只乌鸦跳到她面前的草地上，在那里转着头望着她，然后说道："呱！呱！早安！早安！"乌鸦说话说得很吃力，但还是尽量向格尔达表达自己的想法。乌鸦问她，只身一人在这茫茫无际的大世界旅行感觉怎么样。格尔达听懂了乌鸦说的"只身一人"，对此她体会得太深刻了。于是她把她的全部经历都告诉了乌鸦，并问它见没见到过加伊。

乌鸦若有所思地点点头，说道："可能是他！可能是他！""你真的见到过他吗？"小格尔达叫了起来。她激动地搂住了乌鸦，几乎要把乌鸦勒死了。

"轻点儿！轻点儿！"乌鸦哇哇叫道，"我认为那可能就是加伊！不过他显然因为那位公主就把你忘了！""他和一位公主住在一起吗？"格尔达问。"是的，听我说，我会把一切都告诉你！不过我讲不好你们人类的语言，所以你要有耐心。你要是能听得懂鸟的语言，我就能讲得更明白了！""不好意思，我不懂鸟的语言，"格尔达摇着头说，"但我祖母懂，她也听得懂婴儿的话，我要是也懂得鸟的语言就好了。""没关系！"乌鸦安慰她说，"我会尽量讲清楚，不过我觉得我也许讲不清楚。"

于是乌鸦把它知道的事都讲给了格尔达听。

“在我们现在所处的这个王国里，有位非常聪明的公主。她读过这个世界上所有的报纸，然后就把它们全抛到脑后了，你明白她头脑有多聪明吧？有一天，她厌倦了坐在宝座上的生活，觉得没什么趣味，所以就开始哼唱一首歌，歌词里有一句‘为什么我不结婚呢’。她思考着歌词的含义，就此决定要找个丈夫，但她只想找一个能和她互相交流的人，而不是徒有气派外表的人——因为那样就太无趣了。公主把所有的王室女眷都召集到了一起，和她们讲了自己的想法，她们听完都非常高兴。‘太好了！’她们说，‘前不久我们也想到了这一点。’”

乌鸦注意到格尔达流露出了困惑的表情，于是又解释道：“请你相信，我对你讲的每一个字都是真的！我有个妹妹被人驯养了，她就住在城堡里，这些事都是她告诉我的。就在公主做出决定的第二天，王国所有的报纸都在头版刊登了公主的一张画像，四周装饰着无数颗心。报纸上说的是，邀请所有英俊的年轻男子到城堡与公主面谈，如果有谁能够跟得上公主的思路，对答如流，就会被公主选中！这是真的，是真的！请你相信我！我的话千真万确，与我们现在坐在这里一样真实。很多年轻人蜂拥而至，但是第一天过去了，第二天也过去了，没有人能满足公主的要求。那些年轻人在街上时可以口若悬河，可是只要他们一走进城堡的大门，看到身穿银色制服的警卫，看到身穿金色制服站在最顶层台阶的仆人，他们就开始手足无措了。等到他们来到公主的会客厅时，就变得结结巴巴说不出话，只知道重复公主讲的最后一个词，这当然无法让公主满意啦。就好像这些人一进城堡就昏昏欲眠，回到街上才能清醒过来一样。等待见公主的人从宫殿一直排到城门，长长的队伍望不到尽头。这一点是我亲眼见过的，你一定要相信我！”乌鸦说道，“他们饥渴交加，但是城堡里的人连一杯水都没给他们喝。有些人有先见之明，随身带了面包卷，不过他们不会把面包分给别人吃，他们只盼着其他人都被饿得语无伦次！”

“可是加伊呢，小加伊呢？”格尔达问，“他什么时候来的？他是一个

人来的吗？”“别急！别急！我们就要讲到他了！到了第三天，一个少年出现了。他没骑马，也没乘车，而是大摇大摆地走向城堡。他的眼睛和你的一样闪烁着光彩。他有一头漂亮的长发，不过衣服都快穿烂了！”“那就是加伊！”格尔达高兴地叫道，“啊，这么说我总算找到他了！”她站起身，拍起手来。“他背上背着个包裹！”乌鸦又说。“不是，那一定是他的雪橇！”格尔达纠正道，“因为他是带着雪橇离开家的。”“有可能，”乌鸦说，“我不知道他背上背的是什么！我妹妹告诉我，他走进城堡大门，看到穿银色制服的警卫和台阶上穿金色制服的仆人时，一点儿也不慌张。他朝他们挥了挥手，说，‘像你们这样站在台阶上一定让人厌烦，我宁愿走到里面去’。城堡里烛光明亮，枢密顾问官和大臣们穿着织了金线的天鹅绒便鞋走来走去。我讲这一点是因为，你要知道，大多数人遇到此情此景都会发窘的。那男孩子的靴子发出了很大的嘎吱声，但是他一点儿都没觉得尴尬！”

“这肯定是加伊！”格尔达说，“我知道他离开时穿着双新靴子，他走在路上时我听到了靴子的嘎吱声。”“是的，他的靴子发出了很大的嘎吱声！”乌鸦说，“他平静地径直走到公主面前，公主坐在马车轮子那么大的一颗珍珠上。在她的周围，笔直地站着王室中所有的女子和她们的侍女，以及侍女的侍女，所有的爵士和他们的仆人，以及仆人的仆人。他们站得离门口越近，就越显得高傲！仆人的仆人的小厮平时也总是光着脚的，可是现在几乎让人认不出来，因为小厮紧挨着门口站着，表现出非常骄傲的样子！”“这肯定很吓人啊！”小格尔达说，“但是加伊呢？他娶到公主了吗？”“如果我不是只乌鸦，我也会娶到公主，虽然我已经订过婚。加伊的口才肯定非常好，就像我讲乌鸦话时一样会讲话。这是我妹妹告诉我的。他既勇敢又优雅。他并不是特意来向公主求婚的，他只是听说公主非常有智慧，就想来了解她到底有多聪明，结果他发现她与众不同，而她也发现他与众不同。”

“那肯定就是加伊！”格尔达说，“他是那么聪明，他可以算心算，连小数都能算！哦，你能带我进城堡吗？”“好吧，这说来容易！”乌鸦说，“不过我们怎样才能做得到呢？我要先跟被人驯养了的妹妹商量一下。她能告诉我们该怎么做。现在我只能告诉你，你这样的小女孩一般是不会得到进城堡的许可的。”“我相信我会得到许可的！”格尔达自信地说，“只要加伊知道我来了，马上就会来请我进去的。”“你就在那边的通道等着我吧。”乌鸦说完就张开翅膀飞走了。

直到天已经黑了，乌鸦才飞回来。“呱！呱！呱！”它说，“我代表妹妹问候你。这是我带给你的一小片面包，是从厨房拿出来的，那里有好多面包，你现在肯定饿了。你不可能获准进入城堡，因为你是光着脚的，那些穿银色制服的警卫和穿金色制服的侍者绝对不会让你进去。但是你别哭，还是有办法进去的。我妹妹知道城堡背面有个通往卧室的小门，她会去找找在哪里能弄到钥匙。”

乌鸦带着格尔达进了花园，走过一条林荫大道。枝头的叶子都落了，他们踩在地毯一般的落叶上。

城堡里的灯光一盏接一盏地熄灭以后，乌鸦把小格尔达带到了后门。门是开着的。格尔达感到有点恐慌，同时也充满期待，她的心不禁狂跳起来。她产生了一种奇特的负疚感，觉得这样偷偷溜进城堡是在干坏事，但是她转念一想，自己只不过是希望找到加伊，于是心情又放松下来。来见公主的那个少年一定就是加伊。格尔达回忆起了加伊灵动的眼睛和长长的头发，她仿佛看到加伊就在眼前向她微笑，就和他坐在家里的玫瑰花下朝她微笑时一样。她想，加伊见到她肯定很高兴，她要告诉他，自己为了找他，走过了多么漫长而艰辛的旅程，家里的人担心他遇难了，又是多么难过。想到这些，格尔达真是既害怕又兴奋。

格尔达和乌鸦上了楼梯，看到柜子上点着一盏小灯，屋子中间是那只被人驯养的乌鸦，它正在东张西望，等着格尔达的到来。格尔达按照祖母教的样子行了屈膝礼。

“我的小姑娘，我兄弟说了你很多好话，”被驯养的乌鸦说，“你的故事太感人了！你把灯拿起来好吗？我来给你带路。我们从宫殿这边走，这样就不会碰到别人了。”“我怎么觉得我们身后好像有人跟着呀！”格尔达说。她听到身旁有跑动的声音，墙上似乎有影子飘过，是四肢修长、鬃毛迎风飘动的骏马，还有马车里的绅士和太太。“这些只是梦，”乌鸦对格尔达说，“一到夜里，王子和公主会做到园林里游猎的梦，他们的梦伴随着你，这是件好事，这样你就可以在他们睡觉时好好看看他们了。如果你能因我而获得荣耀和声名，我希望你能有颗感恩的心！”格尔达和乌鸦走进第一个会客厅，墙上挂着粉红色的缎子，上面绣的都是花卉。那些梦从他们身边跑了过去，而且跑得很快，格尔达都没能看清楚那些达官贵人。

他们走过的会客厅一个比一个漂亮，令人眼花缭乱。

乌鸦和小女孩静悄悄地往前走，一直走到了卧室。卧室的天花板就像一棵大棕榈树，上面挂着玻璃做的树叶。在屋子中央，一根大大的金柱子上悬着两张床，每张床都像一朵百合花。其中一张床是白色的，里面睡着公主；另一张床是红色的，格尔达走到这张床边找加伊。她掀起一片红色的花瓣，看到了棕色的脖颈。这肯定是加伊！

她大声喊出了加伊的名字，把灯举到他面前。马背上的梦从客厅里冲了出去，王子醒了，转过头来……啊，他不是加伊！他和加伊一样年轻一样英俊，但是只有脖子像加伊。公主从白色百合花床上起身问是怎么回事。格尔达开始哭泣，讲述了她的全部经历和乌鸦给她的帮助。“啊，可怜的小家伙！”王子和公主齐声说道。他们称赞乌鸦做得对，说他们不但不会生它们的气，反而会给它们奖赏。“你们是愿意自由地飞走呢，还是愿意作为王室的乌鸦留下来，享受吃厨房里所有食物的权利呢？”公主问。两只乌鸦都鞠了一躬，表示愿意接受王室乌鸦的特定角色。王子下了床，请格尔达睡在他的床上，这是他唯一能为她做的。格尔达累坏了，接受了王子的好意。她躺到柔软的床铺上，闭上眼睛，想：“这个王国里的人和动物都是多么善良啊！”几分钟后她就睡熟了。所有的梦都飞了回来，但是这一次它们展现出的景象变了，现在它们拖着个小雪橇，加伊坐在雪橇上挥着手。可惜这一切只不过是场梦，格尔达一醒来，加伊就消失了。

第二天，小姑娘格尔达全身穿上了丝绸和天鹅绒做的新衣服。王子和公主邀请她在城堡里住下来，但她只请求给她一辆小马车、一匹小马和几双小靴子，这样她就又可以继续上路去寻找加伊了。

靴子和暖手筒准备好了，格尔达穿戴好后看上去很漂亮。在她就要离开城堡时，一辆马车停到了城堡门口，那马车是纯金制成的，上面闪耀着王子和公主亮晶晶的徽章。车夫、侍者和骑手都戴着金王冠。王子和公主把格尔达扶上车，祝她有好运气。在林中遇见的那只乌鸦送格尔达走出了三英里。林中乌鸦的妹妹只能在大门口挥动翅膀向格尔达告别。它获得了王室职位后

一下子吃得太多了，现在头疼得厉害，无法出门去送格尔达。金马车内已经备好了甜点，座位上已经摆好了水果和姜汁饼干。

“再会！再会！”王子和公主喊道，林中乌鸦也哭着向格尔达喊再会，格尔达忍不住哭了出来。林中乌鸦飞起来，落到一棵树上，不舍地拍着黑色的翅膀，马车在阳光下闪着金光，越走越远，最后消失在乌鸦的视线之外。

马车金灿灿的光芒惊动了一群强盗，这些强盗一直以密林深处为据点，沿路打劫。“金子！金子！”强盗们嚷嚷着跑过树林，冲到大路上，拦住马车。一场混战之后，骑手、车夫和仆人都成了强盗的俘虏，格尔达也被强盗从车上拖了下来。

“她长得可真美，穿得可真漂亮，她肯定是个贵族，是个王室成员。来吧，让我来准备一场盛宴吧。”一个又丑又老的女强盗边说边从腰带上抽出了一把锈迹斑斑的刀。“哎哟！”这个女强盗突然大叫了一声，原来她女儿趴到了她背上，狠狠咬了她的耳朵一口。“小混蛋！”她喊道。

她女儿却说：“我要她陪我玩！我要她把暖手筒和漂亮衣服都给我。”

说着这孩子又咬了女强盗一口，女强盗疼得跳起来转圈，其他强盗都哄笑起来，说道：“瞧哇，她和她女儿跳舞跳得多好！”

“我要坐那辆金马车！”强盗的女儿说。

这是个固执的、被宠坏了的孩子，想要什么就一定要得到什么。

她和格尔达坐上了马车，驶过干枯的草木和灌木丛，一直跑到树林深处。

强盗的女儿和格尔达个子一样高，不过身体比格尔达强壮结实得多。她的皮肤是棕色的，眼睛黑得像一口深井。她拦腰抱住格尔达，说道：“只要我不生你的气，他们就不能杀你。你是个公主吧？”

“不是。”格尔达回答。她给强盗的女儿讲了自己的奇特经历，也讲了她是多么喜欢加伊。

强盗的女儿神情严肃地看着她，点了点头，又说道：“就算我生你的气，他们也没资格杀你，因为我一定会亲自动手！”她擦干了格尔达的眼泪，把格尔达的双手放进了温暖漂亮的暖手筒里。

马车在强盗城堡的院子中间停了下来。这城堡从上到下布满了裂痕，乌鸦从墙上的各个洞口飞出来飞进去。看门狗跳来跳去，每条狗的体型都特别大，简直能把一个人吞下去。但它们都闷声不响，因为强盗们不让它们叫。

在一个被烟熏黑了的大厅中间，一堆火正熊熊燃烧，上面煮着一大罐子汤，烤肉签子上的兔子肉被烤得劈啪作响。

“今晚你跟我和我所有的小动物一起睡。”强盗的女儿说。

她们吃了些东西，也喝了点汤，然后走到一个角落，那里铺着稻草和毯子。墙上的栖木和板条上落着一百来只鸽子，它们好像都睡着了，不过两个女孩子过来时它们稍稍动了动。“这些都是我的。”强盗的女儿说着快速抓起最近的一只鸽子，提着它的双腿摇了摇，弄得鸽子乱拍起翅膀。“亲它！”她把鸽子推到格尔达脸上，喊道。“这些都是我的鸽子！”她继续说，同时指着墙上用格栅拦着的一个洞。“那两只是野鸽子，如果不把它们关住，它们立刻就会飞走了。这是我最爱的驯鹿。”她抓住一只驯鹿的角，把它拖了过来。驯鹿的鼻子上拴着一个金环。“这家伙也必须牢牢拴住，不然就逃掉了。

每天晚上，我都要用我锋利的刀子在它脖子上搔痒痒来吓唬它。”说完这些冷酷的话，她从墙缝里抽出一把长长的刀，在驯鹿的脖子上蹭了几下。这只可怜的动物开始乱踢。强盗的女儿大笑起来，一下就把格尔达拖上了床。

“你睡觉时总要把这刀放在身边吗？”格尔达惊恐地看着这把长刀，问道。“当然啦！我总是和我的刀一起睡觉！”强盗的女儿回答道，“因为你永远不知道会发生什么意外。不过现在，再给我讲讲你讲过的加伊的事吧，还有你漫游时的经历。”格尔达又把她的故事从头讲了一遍。关在上面的野鸽子咕咕叫着，其他鸽子都睡着了。强盗的女儿一只手拿着刀，也睡着了。不过格尔达无法合眼，她不知道第二天她是会活下去还是会被杀掉。强盗们围着火坐着，边唱歌边喝酒。那个强盗老女人在跳舞。这真是让人心惊肉跳的可怕景象。

这时野鸽子开口说道：“咕！咕！我们见过小加伊。一只大白鸡背着他的雪橇，他坐在冰雪女王的车里，我们在巢里时，车子从树林里穿过去。那时风特别大，所有的小鸟都冻死了，只剩下我们两个。咕！咕！”

“你们说什么？是真的吗？”格尔达轻声问，“冰雪女王去什么地方了？你们知道吗？”

“她肯定是去北极圈附近的拉普兰了，因为那里的冰雪常年不化。你去问问墙边被绳子套着的那只驯鹿吧。”

“那里到处有冰有雪，那里是欢乐的国度！”驯鹿说，“在那里，在明亮的月光下，在宽阔的山谷中，你可以自由地跳跃！那里是冰雪女王在夏天的露营地，但她的城堡坐落在北极附近的一个小岛上，岛的名字叫斯匹茨卑尔根。”

“唉，加伊，小加伊！”格尔达叹了口气。

“别出声！”强盗的女儿咕哝道，“否则我就给你一刀！”

第二天早晨，格尔达把野鸽子的话告诉了强盗的女儿，接着样子非常严肃地扭头问驯鹿：“告诉我，你知道拉普兰在什么地方吗？”

“又有谁能比我知道得更清楚呢？”驯鹿回答，它的眼睛里闪烁着快乐的光芒，“我是在那儿出生，在那儿长大的。我曾在那里的冻土上跳跃。”

“听着！”强盗的女儿对格尔达说，“我们这里的男人都出去了，但我妈妈还留在这里。太阳升起后她总会喝一点儿那个大酒壶里的酒，然后打个盹儿，那时我会帮你个忙！”说完她从床上跳下来，跑到她妈妈那里，扯了扯她的头发，说：“早安，我亲爱的老东西。”她妈妈捏了几下她的鼻子，捏得她鼻子又青又紫，不过这就是她们表达喜爱的方式。老强盗喝光了酒壶里的酒后果然睡着了，强盗的女儿跑到驯鹿面前，说道：“我真想能接着用我锋利的刀给你挠痒痒，因为你太好笑了，不过没关系，我要砍断绳子帮你逃走，让你回到拉普兰。你必须拼命快跑，把这个女孩子带到冰雪女王的城堡去，她的伙伴就在那里。你肯定已经听到她讲的事情了，因为她讲的声音很大，而你一直在竖着耳朵听！”驯鹿高兴得跳了起来，承诺会按她吩咐的做。强盗的女儿帮小格尔达爬到驯鹿背上，给她拿了个小垫子垫着，扶她坐好后又忙着把她和驯鹿牢牢绑到一起，免得她摔下来。“这是你的靴子，”她又嚷道，“天会很冷，你把皮靴穿好，可是我要留下你的暖手筒，因为它太漂亮了！不过我不能让你冻着，这是我母亲的大手套，大概能把你的胳膊肘都套住。你戴上吧！”

格尔达又高兴又感动，泪水忍不住夺眶而出。“我可不喜欢你哭的样子！”强盗的女儿说，“你应该感到开心才对呢！”说完，这个小女孩把一些吃的东西放在驯鹿背上，把门打开，把大狗都关起来，然后用刀割断了拴住驯鹿的绳子，对驯鹿说：“走吧，快跑！不过要照顾好这个小女孩！”格尔达戴好大手套，俯下身拥抱强盗的女儿，和她说了声再会。

驯鹿飞奔出去。它越过灌木丛，穿过树林，跑过草原和沼泽，一刻也不停留地全速奔跑。豺狼在咆哮，乌鸦在尖叫。一道闪光突然划过天空，把整个天空都照亮了，映红了。“那是我最爱的北极光！”驯鹿说，“你快看，它是多么耀眼啊！”驯鹿加快脚步，夜以继日地奔跑着，它完全沉浸在重获自由的欣喜之中，丝毫不知道疲倦。

就这样，他们终于到达了拉普兰。

驯鹿在一间简陋的小屋旁边停了下来。小屋的屋顶几乎和地面连到了一起，门特别矮，住在里面的人需要爬进爬出。屋里只有一个老太太，她正在一盏鲸鱼油灯上煎鱼。格尔达冻得连话都说不出来了，所以驯鹿给老太太讲述了一番格尔达的经历。

“唉，可怜的小家伙！”老奶奶说，“你们还要跑很长的路呢！你们得到芬兰去，大概还要跑一百多英里，因为冰雪女王正在芬兰度假，每天晚上我们都能看到那里的天空被蓝色焰火照得通明。我没有纸，不过我可以在一条干鳕鱼上写个消息，你们可以带着它去芬兰找一位女士，她会给你们提供更详细的消息。”

等到格尔达暖和过来，吃饱喝足之后，拉普兰老太太在一条干鳕鱼上写了两行字，叫格尔达拿好别丢了，然后又把格尔达牢牢绑在驯鹿背上，和她说了再见。空中传来“呼！呼！呼！”的声音，北极光照亮了夜空，陪伴他们奔向目的地。

驯鹿不停地跑。他们终于跑到了要找的芬兰女人家里，敲响了房门。房子里非常热，芬兰女人没穿多少衣服。她赶紧把格尔达的外套、手套和靴子脱下来，不然格尔达在这烧得火热的桑拿房里肯定会热坏的。芬兰女人又在驯鹿头上放了一块冰，然后拿起他们带来的鳕鱼，开始读上面写着的字。她读了三遍，记住了字条的内容之后，就把这条鳕鱼扔进了锅里，因为鳕鱼可以吃，而她是那种从来不浪费任何东西的人。接着她请驯鹿和格尔达讲一讲自己的故事，听的过程中她始终一言不发。

“你是智者，”驯鹿说，“我知道你用一根线就能把世间所有的风都结合在一起，如果水手解开一个结，风就会吹得恰到好处；如果他解开第二个结，风就吹得更厉害；如果他解开第三个和第四个结，就会刮起风暴，树木都会被连根拔起。你可不可以给这个小女孩配一份药水，让她能拥有十二个人的力量，能打败冰雪女王呢？”

“十二个人的力量！”芬兰女人大笑着说，“这有什么好处呢？”然后她走到一个架子那里，取下一大卷兽皮。她把兽皮展开，兽皮上写着奇怪的字母。她仔细读着这些字母，直到汗水顺着额头流了下来。但是驯鹿又一次恳求她帮助格尔达，格尔达自己也眼泪汪汪、充满祈求地看着她。最后芬兰女人决定帮助格尔达。

她把驯鹿牵到角落，在它头上放了一块新鲜的冰，对着它的耳朵轻声说：“小加伊的确和冰雪女王在一起，觉得她那里的一切都符合他的喜好，他认为那里是世界上最美的地方。令他这样想的原因就是，他心中和眼里各有一块魔镜的碎片。必须先把它们取出来，不然他永远都不能长大成人，他会永远对冰雪女王着迷！”

“那你能不能给小格尔达准备一样东西，比如一份药水，或者一个护身符，让她有战胜一切困难的力量呢？”

“她自己本身就拥有强大的力量，我没办法赋予她更多的力量了。你看不出她的力量多么强大吗？你没看到人和动物都在帮助她吗？你没看到她只靠自己的双腿就能走遍世界吗？她是个天真可爱的小姑娘，所以她内心的力量已经足够强大了，她不需要再从我这里获得更多的力量。如果她不能到

冰雪女王那里，把魔镜碎片从小加伊身上取出来，那别人也做不到，这件事我们都无法帮她！冰雪女王的花园离这里大概只有两英里路，你要把她带到那里，把她带到雪地上一处结满红花浆果的大灌木林旁边。不要留在那里闲聊，你必须抓紧时间回到这里！”说着，芬兰女人帮格尔达爬到驯鹿背上，驯鹿又开始全速奔跑。

“哎呀，我没穿靴子！也没戴手套！”小格尔达叫道。她开始觉得冷，可是驯鹿不敢停下来，它一口气跑到结着红色浆果的灌木林旁边，帮助格尔达从它背上跳下来。它流着泪亲了亲格尔达的额头，然后又快速跑回芬兰女人那里。

可怜的格尔达站在芬兰寒冷的雪地上，没有围巾，也没有手套。她拼命往前跑，跑着跑着，她忽然看见了一大片雪花。这些雪花不是从天上落下来的，因为她头上是晴朗宁静的天空。雪花是从园林中间席卷而来的，离她越近就变得越大。格尔达想起她曾透过放大镜看雪花，那些雪花又大又壮美。但是现在她看到的雪花硕大到了可怕的程度，它们张牙舞爪，令人心惊胆战。这些雪花就是冰雪女王的先遣队，是她精心挑选出来的雪花卫士。它们离得越近，格尔达就越能清楚地看到它们怪异的形状，有的像丑陋的肥豪猪，有的像头颈竖起、身子盘成一团的蛇，有的像毛发直立的小胖熊。不论像什么样子，它们全都白得刺眼。

小格尔达哆哆嗦嗦地念了一段祷告词。天太冷了，她能看到自己呼出的白气，烟雾一样的白气越来越浓，渐渐形成了晶莹剔透的小天使。

小天使一落到地面就长大了，每个都戴着头盔。小天使的数目越来越多，格尔达念完祷告词以后，周围已经出现了一个天使兵团。这些小天使挥剑向可怕的雪花卫士砍去，把雪花砍成无数碎片，于是小格尔达就能安全自信地前进了；他们轻触格尔达的手和脚，这样她在朝着冰雪女王的城堡进发时就不会觉得那么冷了。

不过我们还是先来看看加伊在做什么吧。

自从他追随冰雪女王以来，在漫长的日子里，他从来都没想到过小格尔达，一次都没想到过。冰雪女王的吻抹去了他头脑中对朋友的记忆，也抹去了他心中对朋友的挂念。就算他知道小格尔达为了寻找他走了那么远的路，也丝毫不会为之所动。此时的他也根本想不到，格尔达已经穿过了层层冰雪的大门，走进了冰雪女王的城堡。

小女孩格尔达焦急地迈入城堡。她抬头环视四周，眼前的一切让她屏住了呼吸。

宫殿的墙是用积雪筑成的，窗户和门是风吹在雪上形成的。她前面是长长的楼梯，冰块雕成的台阶通往二楼，那里有一百多个房间，房间的大小是由落下多少雪花决定的，其中最大的房间的长度竟然有好几英里。

北极光照亮了所有房间，每个房间都又大又空旷，冷冰冰、亮晶晶的。这里是欢乐从不涉足的地方。这里从来不会举办北极熊的舞会，也不会邀请小白狐姑娘们来开宴会。冰雪女王的这些大房间全都空空荡荡，冰冰冷冷。

格尔达穿过城堡最高层那长长的走廊，来到最后一个冰雪大厅，看到大厅中央有个结了冰的湖。湖面破裂成了一千片碎片，每一片都和其他碎片形状相同，冰湖本身就是一件艺术品。冰湖的中央放着冰雪女王的宝座，小加伊每天都坐在冰湖中央，他的脸和手都冻成了青紫色，看上去简直都发黑了，但他自己不会觉得冷，因为冰雪女王除掉了他感知寒冷的能力，让他的心像冰块一样坚硬。

格尔达看到加伊时，加伊就坐在宝座下面，挪动着几块平整而带尖角的冰块，把它们摆来摆去，想拼成他想要的图案，就像拼积木一样。

在加伊眼中，他拼出的各种形状都妙不可言，意义非凡，而这完全是因为他眼睛里的那块魔镜碎片。

接着他又想用这些冰块拼出一个词——“永恒”，但是怎么也拼不出来。冰雪女王曾对他说：“如果你能拼出这个词，那你就是你自己的主人了，我会给你整个世界和一双新鞋子。”可是加伊一直拼不出来。每次他努力拼这个词时，那些碎冰块都会滑到一旁，离开其他冰块，仿佛它们有自己的意识一样。

“我得走了，”冰雪女王对加伊说，“我必须去温暖的国度，看看我那些大黑锅！”她指的是那些火山，那些在冬季也处于她管辖范围内的神奇山峰。“我必须去给它们涂上点儿白色！现在正是时候，柠檬和葡萄上的雪看起来会非常漂亮。”冰雪女王说完就飞走了。

加伊独自一人留在拱顶覆盖着冰块的宽敞房间里，摆弄着他的那些冰块。他仍然一心想要拼出“永恒”这个词，想得他的头都要炸开了。他一动不动，僵硬地坐在那里，看上去就像被冻死了。小格尔达就是在这时看到加伊的，她朝加伊跑去。

跑到加伊身边时，格尔达搂着他的脖子，用力拥抱他，嘴里喊道：

“加伊，亲爱的小加伊！我终于找到你了！”

加伊却一动不动，僵硬地坐在那里，就像被冻住了。小格尔达难过得流下了热泪。炽热的泪水落到加伊的胸膛上，渗进加伊的心里，把里面那块魔镜碎片融化了。加伊望着她，突然哭了起来。他哭得很厉害，眼泪把眼睛中的镜子碎屑冲了出来，于是他高兴地叫道：“格尔达，亲爱的小格尔达！这段时间你都在哪里呀？我这又是在哪里呀？”他害怕地望着周围。“这里真冷啊！真大真空旷啊！”

他抱着格尔达，紧紧地搂着她。格尔达高兴得又哭又笑。这情景太美妙了，连周围的冰块都快乐地围着他们跳起舞来，直到累得没力气才停下。那些冰块形成的图案，正是冰雪女王要加伊拼出的那个词——“永恒”。

冰雪女王曾说，如果加伊能拼出“永恒”这个词，他就会成为自己的主人，并且赢得整个世界和一双新鞋子。

格尔达亲吻着加伊的脸颊，现在他的脸颊又有了血色；格尔达亲吻着加伊的眼睛，现在他的眼睛又和她的一样明亮了；格尔达亲吻着加伊的手，他发自内心地大笑起来。

冰雪女王现在回来也无妨了，在她的宝座下面，亮闪闪的冰块已经拼出了“再见”。格尔达和加伊手挽着手，离开了巨大的城堡。

外面风停了，太阳出来了，他们不停地向对方述说着，说起了祖母、屋顶上的玫瑰花，还有他们到过的地方。他们来到结着红色浆果的灌木丛旁，发现送格尔达来的驯鹿和另外一头驯鹿一起在那里等着他们。两头驯鹿先是把加伊和格尔达送到了芬兰女人那里。他们在她温暖的房间里暖和过来，从她那里知道了回家的路要怎么走。然后他们到了拉普兰女人那里，她已经为他们缝好了新衣服，还给了他们一架雪橇。两头驯鹿在拉普兰女人身边跳来跳去，一直把格尔达和加伊送到拉普兰的边境，那里的草已经冒出了春天的绿芽。他们互相告别，每个人都说着“再会”。

格尔达和加伊沿着大路走进一片树林。从一棵大橡树后面跑出来一匹马，那是一匹拉过金马车的骏马。马背上坐着个女孩，她头戴漂亮的红帽子，双手各拿着一把手枪。她正是强盗的女儿。她厌倦了守在家里，想先去北方，再去其他地方探险。她和格尔达立刻认出了对方，两个人都非常高兴。加伊说：“你要周游世界呀，真是潇洒！”她回答道：“我倒想知道，你值不值得让人跑到世界尽头去寻找。”不过格尔达拍了拍加伊的脸，向强盗的女儿问起了那位王子和公主的情况。“他们都去外国旅行了！”强盗的女儿说。“那只乌鸦还好吗？”格尔达问道。“唉，听说那只乌鸦已经死了，它妹妹在腿上系了根黑线，走到哪里都伤心地悼念它！不过这都是我听说的。现在给我讲讲你离开后的经历吧。”格尔达和加伊讲了他们的经历，强盗的女儿听完后拥抱了他们，答应说如果有一天她能路过他们的城市，一定会去拜访他们。然后她就骑着马奔向那茫茫无边的未知世界了。

格尔达和加伊手挽着手继续往前走。他们所到之处都是一片春光，鲜花盛开，绿草茵茵。两个人一路走一路说笑。他们走啊走，最后终于望见了教堂的尖塔，那是他们的家所在的城市。他们走进城，一直走到祖母家的门口；他们爬上楼梯，走进房间，一切都和他们离开时一样，然而就在打开房门的那一刻，他们发现自己已经是大人了。

种在集水沟上的玫瑰花正在盛开，花枝伸进了敞开的窗户。格尔达和加伊年少时坐过的椅子还在那里，两人在椅子上坐下来，执手相视。他们已经不再去回想冰雪女王的宫殿里那凄冷、壮观、空空荡荡的景象了，那一切就像一场被人遗忘的噩梦。他们坐在那里，两个人虽然都已经长大，但内心依然是纯真的孩子。

炎热的夏季终于到来了……

图书在版编目（CIP）数据

冰雪女王 /（意）曼纽拉·阿德雷亚尼绘；（丹）安徒生著；李静滢译. —广州：广东人民出版社，2023.3

（镜子书·新编经典童话绘本系列）
ISBN 978-7-218-16035-1

Ⅰ. ①冰… Ⅱ. ①曼… ②安… ③李… Ⅲ. ①儿童故事—图画故事—意大利—现代 Ⅳ. ① I546.85

中国版本图书馆 CIP 数据核字（2022）第 175729 号

BINGXUE NÜWANG
冰 雪 女 王
［意］曼纽拉·阿德雷亚尼 绘 ［丹］安徒生 著 李静滢 译

出 版 人：肖风华

责任编辑：寇 毅
责任技编：吴彦斌 周星奎

出版发行：广东人民出版社
地 址：广州市越秀区大沙头四马路 10 号（邮政编码：510199）
电 话：（020）85716809（总编室）
传 真：（020）83289585
网 址：http://www.gdpph.com
印 刷：北京尚唐印刷包装有限公司
开 本：1000 毫米 ×1250 毫米 1/16
印 张：5 **字 数**：46 千
版 次：2023 年 3 月第 1 版
印 次：2023 年 3 月第 1 次印刷
定 价：78.00 元

如发现印装质量问题，影响阅读，请与出版社（020-87712513）**联系调换。**
售书热线：（020）87717307

创美工厂®

出 品 人：许　永
出版统筹：林园林
责任编辑：寇　毅
特邀编辑：陈璐璟
装帧设计：李嘉木
印制总监：蒋　波
发行总监：田峰峥

发　　行：北京创美汇品图书有限公司
发行热线：010-59799930
投稿信箱：cmsdbj@163.com

官方微博

微信公众号

THE SNOW QUEEN

BASED ON THE MASTERPIECE BY

HANS CHRISTIAN ANDERSEN

ILLUSTRATIONS BY

MANUELA ADREANI

Are you ready? We are about to tell you a very, very scary story that started because of an evil spirit, one of the worst: the devil. One day he succeeded in doing something very bad, and that made him feel very good. Making use of his knowledge of the black arts, he built a mirror that could conceal all the beautiful and good things reflected in it, showing only a different, horrible side; and on the other hand what was already ugly and bad became even worse. As a result, the most beautiful landscapes were transformed into cooked spinach and the faces of the best people were flattened as if pressed against glass or deformed by a terrible grimace to the point of becoming unrecognizable. The smallest defects became grossly exaggerated and if, for example, someone had a single freckle, you could be sure that it would become so large as to cover the entire face. It was really very amusing, said the devil. If anyone was having a good thought the mirror would transform it into an evil one: with such results the devil was bound to find his terrible invention extremely satisfying.

All the witches who went to the devil's school of black magic said in turn that they had witnessed a miracle: through the magic mirror they could now at last see the world and human beings as they really should have been. Together they traveled all over the

world with the mirror and in the end there was not a single country or a single person who had not been reflected and deformed in the mirror. But one wicked action always led to another, so, still not satisfied, they decided to fly to heaven and make fun of the angels. They carried the mirror up to heaven, then they burst out laughing so much at the mischief they were about to commit that, shaking with glee, they found it difficult to keep holding the mirror. They had almost reached the place in heaven where the angels were gathered when suddenly the mirror shook so much because of their laughter that they dropped it and it fell back to earth, where it broke into a million pieces or more. So it did even more damage than before, because some of the pieces were as small as grains of sand, and these traveled to the four corners of the earth, blown by the high spirited spring wind. Then when the grains of sand got into people's eyes they remained there, so that people saw everything distorted, or they only managed to see the worst side of things, because each tiny piece of the mirror had the same power as that terrible object had had before it was broken.

Some tiny splinters of the mirror entered people's hearts and this was really horrible: the heart became like a piece of ice.
Some pieces, on the other hand, were so large that they were used to make window panes by ignorant glaziers, but whoever looked at the outside world through these windows saw it as horrible and cruel, inhabited by monstrous creatures, so they remained barricaded at home for the rest of their lives! Other pieces were used to make spectacles, and this was really terrible, because usually people used their glasses to see better and to see things fairly, but obviously this was no longer possible. The devil laughed so much that his stomach wobbled and tickled, while the fragments of mirror continued to fly through the air.
Now that you know how the mirror came into existence, let us hear what happened next.
In the big city the houses and people were packed so tightly together that there was no room left for gardens, so most people had to make do with flowers in vases. But in the poor area where the two children who are the heroes of our story lived, using a little imagination it had been possible to create a tiny garden, hardly bigger than a vase of flowers.

The houses of their parents were so close to each other that where the roofs adjoined the gutters were touching: you could walk across them to go from one attic to the other, through the little windows in the roof. The parents had put large wooden flower boxes outside the windows of each house. In them they grew aromatic herbs to use in the kitchen as well as a tiny rose garden; there was one rose in each box and they were both growing very well. One day the parents thought of arranging the boxes across the gutters so that they almost joined the two windows, thus creating an embankment of flowers. The sweet peas hung down gracefully while the roses grew taller and climbed round the windows, forming a triumphal arch of flowers and greenery. Because the boxes were very high, the children were allowed to climb out of the window so they could sit on their little seats beneath the roses and play there blissfully. So they spent the spring and summer enjoying themselves, but in winter the rose bushes were bare and the windows were frozen. Then the children heated a copper coin and placed it on each frozen window in turn, so as to make little round peep-holes through which a bright eye would sparkle, one from each window: they were the eyes of the children, who liked to keep in touch with each other. They were not brother and sister but they might as well have been, and they did not like spend too much time apart.

He was called Kay and she was called Gerda.

While in the summer they could get together with just a jump, in winter they had to get out of the house, going down lots of stairs and then climbing up as many again, even during snowstorm and blizzards.

"They are not snowflakes but white bees that are swarming!" the old grandmother said at the time. "Do they also a have queen bee?" the little boy asked, because he knew that with real bees there was always a queen. "Of course they have a queen!" the old woman replied. "She flies there where the bees are flying in a dense swarm! She is larger than all the other bees and she never lands on the ground, but when she gets close, she flies high up again into the dark sky. On many winter nights she flies through the streets of the city and looks in through the windows, then the windows ice up in the strangest way, as if they were covered with flowers. At this point the children cried out together: "Yes, I have seen that!" and then they knew that she was telling the truth. "Can the Snow Queen get in here?" the little girl asked. "Let her come!" the little boy replied, "I shall put her on the hot stove so that she melts."

But the grandmother, gently stroking their hair, changed the subject and told them other stories. One evening little Kay, already half undressed, climbed onto a chair near the window and, look-

ing through the little peep-hole, he saw two large snow flakes drifting towards him. One of them, the larger one, came to rest on the corner of one of the flower boxes. It started to grow bigger and bigger until it finally turned into a tall woman, wrapped in very fine white veils that looked as if they were created by a swirling snowstorm. She was very beautiful and elegant but made of ice, resplendent and sparkling ice, like the stars, but she was alive; she was staring in front of her but her eyes did not express peace and serenity. She made a gesture towards the window and greeted Kay with a slow wave of her hand. Kay was terrified and jumped off the seat, while on the other side of the window a whirlwind transformed the woman into a large white bird that flapped its wings and flew away.

When Kay woke up in the morning he saw that that during the night all the houses in the street had been covered with a thick blanket of ice. But as it did every year, later the ice began to thaw, then spring arrived, the sun shone, the plants grew, the swallows built their nests, the windows were opened and the children returned to their old habit of meeting in their little garden. That summer the roses were wonderful: the children held hands, admiring the buds that had developed during the night while enjoying the warmth of the sun. Such wonderful summer days, it was so lovely to be outside, next to those magnificent roses that never

seemed to want to stop flowering.

One day while Kay and Gerda were looking at a picture book of animals and birds, just as the bell of the large church tower struck five in the afternoon, Kay suddenly cried out: "Ouch! I felt a stab in my heart and something got in my eye!" The little girl held his head to help him get it out while he blinked his eyes, but no, she could not see anything. "I think it must have come out," Gerda said, but she was wrong. Something much more serious had happened:

IT WAS ONE OF THE TINY SPLINTERS OF GLASS FROM THE MIRROR, FROM THE MAGIC MIRROR: DO YOU REMEMBER IT, THE HORRIBLE MIRROR THAT MADE ALL GREAT AND GOOD THINGS LOOK TINY AND HORRIBLE, WHILE EVIL, NASTY THINGS LOOKED EVEN WORSE?

Poor Kay, a tiny piece of that mirror had got into his eye and descended to his heart, where it would soon become like a lump of ice!

It was true that it did not hurt any more, but the piece of mirror was still there.

"Why are you crying?" Kay asked Gerda, suddenly getting angry without reason. "You are ugly when you cry, and anyway, there is

nothing wrong with me!" Then out of the blue he shouted: "Uh! That rose has been nibbled by a worm! And look, the other one is all deformed! In fact all these roses are horrible! They look worse than the boxes in which they are planted!" Then he kicked the window box violently and tore off two roses.

"Kay! What are you doing?" the little girl cried out, but when he saw how frightened she was, he tore off another rose and ran away through his window, far away from kind Gerda.

Later, when Gerda went to his house to make friends again, with a picture book in her hands, he told her sharply that the book was for children. And when the grandmother started telling them fairy tales as she always did after dinner in the evening, Kay interrupted her with a "So?" Then he began walking behind her, snatched her glasses and mimicked her. He was very good at imitating her and from then on he also did it in the street, where people saw him and laughed. Soon he was imitating all the neighbors. Any detail or feature in them that was strange or ugly, Kay would imitate, and he did this so well that people said: "He's very smart, that boy!" But in fact, all this was happening because of the piece of mirror that had got in his eye and then into his heart: this was why he was behaving as he did, even poking fun at poor little Gerda.

When winter arrived, his games were very different from those of the previous year. One day when it was snowing very hard, Kay arrived with large magnifying glass and dangled the hem of his blue jacket out of the window, waiting for the snow flakes to cover it. "Look through this magnifying glass, little Gerda!" he said showing her how, through the magnifying glass, each snow-flake became much bigger, looking like a wonderful flower or a ten-pointed star. " You see how beautiful it is? It is perfect!" Kay said. "This is interesting, not like those stupid roses. These flakes are perfect, do you see? They are all identical. If only they would not melt..." Without waiting for the little girl's reply, he returned home, then he went out again wearing thick gloves and carrying a little sledge on his back.

"Where are you going, Kay?" Gerda shouted.

"To the main square where the other boys are playing!" he replied as he turned the corner.

On the square the most reckless of the boys would tie their sledges to people's carts without them knowing. Then when the cart set off, the boys were pulled along for a good distance: they found this very entertaining! They were having great fun doing this when a large sledge arrived, all painted white. Sitting in it was a person wrapped up in soft, white fur, her face covered by a hood. The sledge went round the square twice, then stopped in the middle.

Kay took the opportunity of getting close to the white sledge without being seen and tied his sledge to it so he would be pulled along. He had just finished tying the last knot when, as if by an agreed signal, the sledge set off, going faster and faster, travelling through the roads and streets at great speed without hesitation. The person who was driving the sledge so skillfully greeted Kay with an affectionate nod of the head as if they already knew each other. Kay was terrified and every time he tried to undo the knots, the person nodded at him again, so Kay remained clinging to his sledge with all his might until, moving at a crazy speed, they reached the city gate. At this point the snow started falling so thickly that Kay could see no more than a few inches in front of him as he was dragged along. Once again he tried to undo the rope but in vain: the rope was completely frozen. He then screamed loudly but no one heard him. The snow went on falling, the wind went on blowing and the sledge went on racing, as fast as the wind, jolting now and again as if it was jumping over hedges and ditches.

Kay was terrified, he wanted to pray but he could only remember his multiplication tables!

The snow flakes were becoming ever larger until they looked like big white birds. Suddenly the sledge jumped to one side and stopped. The driver got up and removed her hood, thus revealing her face. First Kay noticed that the white fur in which she was wrapped was in fact snow, then he looked up and recognized her: she was a tall, slender woman, a vision of glittering whiteness. It was the Snow Queen.

"We've had a good ride!" the lady exclaimed with an icy smile, "but it is really cold, you must be frozen! Come here and take shelter in my bear fur!" Still smiling, the lady took Kay by the hand and led him to the sledge where she made him sit next to her seat. Having wrapped himself in her fur, the boy felt as if he was sinking into a mountain of snow. "Are you still cold?" she asked, then kissed him on the forehead. Oh! the kiss was colder than the ice, and it went straight to his heart, which was already frozen. He felt as if he was dying, but only for a brief moment, then he felt well again and was no longer aware of the cold that had made him shiver until a moment earlier.

The first thing he remembered and said was "The little sledge! Don't forget my little sledge!" But the Snow Queen gave him another kiss and suddenly he forgot little Gerda and all the other people he had left behind.

"I shall not kiss you any more!" the queen cried out laughing, "otherwise I would make you die." Kay looked at her: she was so beautiful! He could never have imagined a more fascinating, intelligent face. Now it no longer seemed to made of ice, as it

had when he had seen her outside his window and she had waved at him. In his eyes she was perfect and he no longer felt afraid. Feeling perfectly at ease with her, her told he was good at mental arithmetic and also at fractions, that he knew the area in square miles of many countries and the number of their inhabitants, and all the time she continued smiling at him.

Then Kay thought that his knowledge might not be enough, so he told her this and asked her to show him something new. The queen nodded, looked up and, without a gesture or a word, she made the carriage fly through the air, travelling through the furious, howling snowstorm with the greatest of ease.

They flew over woods and lakes, gardens and villages. Meanwhile below them, the cold wind was whistling, the wolves were howling and the snow was falling, and above them black cawing ravens were flying and the moon shone, large and luminous through the long, long winter night.

When day broke Kay was sleeping at the feet of the Snow Queen.

You can imagine how little Gerda felt when Kay did not return! Where had he ended up? The little girl could think of nothing else and she asked all the people in the city, but no one could tell her. Some of the boys who had been playing with him that day on the hill only remembered seeing him tie his little sledge to a larger one that had stopped in the square, then left through the city gate, but they weren't absolutely certain of this: their memory was inexplicably confused, as if shrouded in thick fog. The only thing they remembered very clearly was that the temperature had suddenly dropped so much that they had gone home, completely frozen. In short, no one knew where the boy had gone or with whom he had gone away… Many tears were shed on the days that followed, and you can be sure that little Gerda cried her heart out longer than anyone when they said that Kay must have drowned in the river that flowed by the city.

It was the longest and saddest winter that the little girl had ever experienced, but even that year spring and its warm sun arrived. Gerda went into the garden where she and Kay used to spend wonderful days together, she looked at the roses that were beginning to flower, then she looked up at the spring sun and suddenly she spoke: "Kay has drowned," she said, and dried a tear.

"No, I do not believe it!" the sun replied incredulously.

"I tell you he is dead, he has disappeared!" Gerda replied as some swallows flew past.

"We do not believe it!" they replied and so, in the end, little Gerda no longer believed it either.

"I shall put on my new red shoes," she decided one morning, "the ones that Kay has never seen before, and I shall go to the river and ask about him." She was very quick and the old grandmother

was still asleep, so Gerda decided not to wake her. She kissed her gently on her forehead and said goodbye; then she put on her red shoes and left the city on her own, determined to go to the river and to discover the truth about her friend.

"Have you taken Kay?" she asked the river. "I shall give you my red shoes if you let him come home." It seemed to her that the waves were making strange signs, so she took her red shoes, the ones she loved more than any others, and threw them into the river, but the waves immediately threw them back onto the bank. It seemed as if the river did not want to take what Gerda loved most, perhaps because it knew it could not give Kay back to her; but the little girl thought that possibly she had not thrown the shoes far enough into the river, so she climbed into a boat she found among the reeds, walked to prow, and from there she threw the shoes in the river. But the boat had not been properly tied up and by walking on it she had made it move away from the jetty so that it was now slowly drifting away from the shore.

Gerda noticed this and immediately tried to get out, but before she could do so the boat had moved too far away from the bank and, propelled by the current, it was traveling faster and faster.

Little Gerda was terrified and started crying; no one heard her except the sparrows, but they could not help her get back on land. So they decided to accompany her, singing as they flew, as if to say: "We are here! We are here!"

The boat sailed down the river with little Gerda sitting in it barefoot: her red shoes were bobbing behind the boat but they never managed to catch up with it because it was moving too fast.

The river banks were very beautiful, lined with lovely flowers and shaded by old trees, but there was not a soul to be seen.

"Perhaps the river will take me to Kay," she thought, and this made her happy again and no longer afraid; she sat up and admired the countryside she was travelling through, until she reached a cottage with strange red and blue windows, a thatched roof and a beautiful front garden with large cherry trees.

The river was driving the boat towards the shore, so Gerda shouted and gesticulated until a very old woman emerged from the cottage. She was wearing a large straw hat decorated with flowers and leant on a crook as she approached the river.

"Oh, poor little girl," she exclaimed when she saw Gerda. "What did you do to get caught in this strong current and dragged so far from any city?" As she spoke she walked into the water, caught the boat with her crook, pulled it to the river bank and helped the little girl get out.

Gerda was happy to find herself on dry land again but she was a little scared of this old woman whom she did not know, who now asked her: "Come, tell me how you arrived here."

Gerda told her everything while the old lady shook her head saying: "Hum! Hum!" After finishing her story, Gerda asked her if by any chance she had seen little Kay, and the woman replied that he would surely come this way. Then she told the little girl not to be sad but instead to make herself comfortable in the house and rest while enjoying some cherries and admiring her flowers, which were much more beautiful than the ones in picture books, because each one of them could tell a story. The old lady took Gerda by the hand and led her inside the cottage, then she locked the door.

The windows were very high and the panes were red, blue and yellow. The daylight streaming in was completely transformed by these colors, while on the table were some beautiful bright red cherries. Gerda was so hungry that she ate two handfuls, and then she was no longer afraid.

Meanwhile with a gold comb the old woman began combing the golden curls framing the little girl's pretty round face.

"I have always wanted a sweet little girl like you!" the old woman exclaimed. "You will see how happy the two of us will be together."

While the old woman was combing her hair, little Gerda forgot about Kay, because the old woman was a witch. She was not a bad witch, her spells were quite innocent and all she wanted now

was to keep little Gerda with her so as not to be alone anymore.

When she saw that the little girl was relaxed, she went into the garden and pointed her crook at all the rose bushes that were covered in flowers and made them all disappear into the black earth until it was impossible to know that they had ever been there. The witch was afraid that, if she saw the roses, Gerda would think of her own ones, then remember little Kay and run away. After making the roses disappear, she let the little girl go into the flower garden.

Gerda came out of the cottage and opened her eyes wide: what beauty, what wonderful fragrance! All the flowers imaginable were there and they were all flowering.

Gerda thought that the witch was right: no picture book could more beautiful or more colorful. The little girl jumped for joy and played in the garden until the sun set behind the big cherry trees, then the witch accompanied her to a room that would be her very own bedroom, where Gerda found a lovely little bed with covers of pink silk, embroidered with blue violets. She slept soundly and had happy dreams, better than any queen would have had even on her wedding day. When she woke up the next morning, she went out to play in the sun again, with the flowers, and she did the same thing again the next day and the day after. After a few months Gerda could recognize every flower, but every time she went into the garden she stopped, perplexed, to look at the large empty flower bed from which the roses had disappeared, feeling that something was missing there. One day she found herself looking closely at the witch's old straw hat, decorated with drawings of thousands of colorful flowers, the most beautiful of which was a rose. The old woman had forgotten to remove it from her hat when she buried all the others in the earth. Well, you can't think of everything!

"How is this possible!" Gerda cried out, "when there isn't even a single rose bush in the garden?" She jumped among the flower beds, looking and looking, but she could not find any; then she sat down and cried because she was so disappointed and her tears fell exactly where the rose garden had been buried. When her tears fell on the earth, wetting it, a rose bush suddenly emerged from the earth, flowering as it had been when it was buried. Gerda put her arms round the rose bush, then looking at the roses, she suddenly remembered the ones in the window box back home and so she thought of little Kay again. "Oh, I have lost so much time!" the little girl said to herself. "I must find Kay! Do you

know where I could find him?" she asked the roses. "Do you think he is dead?"

"No, he is not dead", the flowers replied. "We are certain of it!"

"Thank you! But where can I find him?" Gerda asked all the flowers in the garden but none had an answer: they were in the sun, dreaming about fairy tales or the stories that the earth or the wind were telling them.

The first to speak was the red lily, and it said: "Do you hear the drum? Boom! Boom! There are only two notes, always boom! boom! Can you hear the sound of women wailing with sorrow? Can the flame in the heart die in the flame of the funeral pyre?"

"I don't understand a word you are saying!" confessed little Gerda. "It's my story!" the offended red lily replied.

"What does the morning glory say?

"There at the end of a narrow mountain road is an ancient fortress; thick green ivy covers its old red walls, leaf by leaf, up around the balcony, where there is a beautiful girl who is leaning over the parapet and looking towards the road." said the flower. "No rose growing among the branches has a fresher complexion than her, no apple blossom blown from the tree by the wind is lighter than her; listen to the rustling of her magnificent silk robe! He is not yet come!" it added sadly.

"Do you mean Kay?" little Gerda asked. "What does the little

primrose have to say?"

"A long plank hangs from a branch, tied to the tree with two ropes: it is a see-saw! Two graceful young girls, dressed all in white like snow with long green silk ribbons in their hair are rocking on it; their brother, who is older than them, is standing on the see-saw and holding the rope with his arm, because in one hand he has a little bowl and in the other a straw with which he is blowing soap bubbles. The see-saw is rocking and the shimmering soap bubbles keep flying away in the air; the last bubble is still attached to the straw and then it is blown away by the wind; the see-saw continues rocking. The black puppy, as light as the bubbles, is standing on its hind legs and it wants to get on the see-saw too; but the see-saw is rocking and the puppy falls, barks and gets angry; it is disappointed as the bubbles burst. A plank swinging, an image of bursting soap bubbles, this is my song!"

"Your story may be beautiful, but you tell it with such sadness and you do not mention Kay. What do the hyacinths say?"

"Once upon a time there were three very beautiful sisters, pale and slender, one dressed in red, the next in blue and the third in white; they were holding hands and dancing in the moonlight near the peaceful little lake. They were not elves, they were daughters of men. There was a wonderfully sweet fragrance, and the girls disappeared into the wood while the bright fireflies flew

all around, like delicate little lights."

"You make me so sad !" said little Gerda, "You have such a strong perfume, I…"

"Ding, dong, ding, dong," the bells of the hyacinths interrupted her. "We are not ringing for little Kay, we do not even know him! We are just singing our own song, the only one we know!"

Gerda then walked towards the buttercup, shining among its bright green leaves. "You are like a little sun," she said. "Tell me if you know where I can find my playmate!" And the buttercup sparkled as it looked at Gerda. What song could it sing? But this song did not mention Kay either.

The warm sun of the first day of spring was shining in a little courtyard. Its rays were falling on the white wall of the neighboring house at the foot of which the first yellow flowers were growing, sparkling like gold. The old grandmother was outside on her chair when her little granddaughter, a poor but pretty housemaid, came to the house for a short visit. As soon as she arrived she greeted her grandmother with a kiss. There was gold in that loving kiss, the pure gold of the heart. Gold on the mouth, gold at the bottom of the heart, gold here in the first hours of the morning! That is my little story!" said the buttercup.

"It is talking about my poor old grandmother!" Gerda sighed. "She certainly misses me, and she is sad like I was for little Kay,

but I shall return home soon and bring Kay back with me. It is no use asking the flowers, they only know their own songs." She held up her dress to run faster, but the narcissus caught her leg while she was jumping over it; then Gerda stopped, looked at long yellow stem and asked the flower: "Perhaps you know something?" and she bent down to touch it. What was the narcissus saying? Winding itself round Gerda's shoulders, it told her a strange story: "I can see myself, I can see myself!" the narcissus said. "Up in the little attic, half-dressed, is a little ballerina, standing sometimes on one leg, sometimes on two; she is kicking out at the whole world, but it is only an illusion. She pours the water in the teapot onto a piece of fabric that she is holding in her hand: it is her bodice.The white dress that is hanging from the hook is also washed in the water of the teapot and then put on the roof to dry. Then she puts the dress on, with a tiny scarf as yellow as saffron round her neck, to set off the whiteness of her dress. Leg up in the air! See how she stands on one leg! I can see myself! I can see myself!"

"I'm not interested in anything you are saying!" Gerda cried out exasperated. "They are not things you should be telling me!" she added, running towards the garden fence. The gate was closed, but she lifted the rusty hook, so the gate opened and she ran barefoot into the street. Three times she looked behind her, but no

one was following her. When she was exhausted and could not run any more, she sat down on a large stone and looked around her. Summer was over, it was already late autumn, but she had not noticed this in the beautiful garden where the sun was always shining and there were flowers in all seasons. "Oh, I'm late! It's already autumn: now I cannot even have a rest!" little Gerda cried out, and she got up to set off again. Her little feet were tired and hurting and she was surrounded by cold and sadness. The long leaves of the willows were all yellow, covered in hoar frost. The leaves were falling one after the other, only the plum tree still had fruit on it, but the plums were so bitter that they made the teeth tingle. How grey and sad the world was!

When Gerda had to stop again to rest, a large crow jumped on the snow right in front of her and remained there watching her, shaking his head; then he said: "Caw, caw! Good morning, good morning!" He did not speak very well but he made a big effort and asked the girl how it was that she was traveling the big wide world all on her own. The word "alone", this Gerda understood, because she knew very well what it meant. So she told the crow the story of her life and asked him if he had seen Kay. The bird moved his head thoughtfully and said: "It could be! It could be!"

"Do you really think so?" little Gerda cried out, hugging him so enthusiastically as to hurt him.

"Slow down, slow down!" croaked the crow. "I think it might be little Kay, but he has certainly forgotten you in favor of the princess!"

"He lives with a princess?" Gerda asked.

"Yes, listen, I shall explain everything! You must be patient because I do not speak your language very well. If you knew the language of birds, it would be much easier!"

"No, I'm sorry, I don't know it." said Gerda said shaking her head, "but my grandmother knows it and she also knows the language of the newborn. If only I had learnt it too!"

"It doesn't matter!" the crow reassured her, "I shall speak as best I can, although I am sure I shall explain it badly." Having said this, the bird started telling Gerda what he knew. "In this kingdom, where we are now, there lives an extraordinarily intelligent princess: she reads all the newspapers of the world and then she forgets them, do you understand how clever her mind is? One day, being bored just sitting there on her throne, which is not very entertaining, she started singing a song that included the words: 'Why should I not get married?' Reflecting on the words of the song, she decided to find a husband, but she only wanted one who would take part in conversation, not someone who was merely grand and distinguished, because that would be very dull. The princess gathered all the ladies of the court around her, and

when they heard what she wanted they were extremely pleased. 'Very good!' they said, 'we were just thinking about that only the other day.' Know that you can believe every word I tell you!" the crow added when he noticed Gerda' s bemused expression. "My sister is tame and lives in the castle: she has told me all this. The following day all the newspapers in the kingdom were published with the symbol of the princess on the front page and borders decorated with a thousand hearts. The newspaper said that all good-looking young men were invited to go the castle and talk with the princess. Those who proved capable of keeping up with her conversation would be chosen by the princess! Yes, yes, you can believe me, it is really true, as true as we are sitting here. Young men flocked to the castle in large numbers! But the matter was not resolved, not on the first day, nor on the second. They could all speak very well when they were still on the street, but as soon as they had gone through the castle gate and saw the guards with their silver uniform, and at the top of the stairs the valets dressed in a gold livery, they became confused. So when they found themselves in the throne room they were unable to open their mouths except to repeat the princess's last word, and of course that did not interest her at all! It was as if people became half-asleep on entering the castle and woke up again when back on the street! There was an endless queue that ran from the city gates to the palace. You must believe me, I saw it myself," said the crow. "They were all hungry and thirsty, but no one from the castle gave them even a glass of water. Admittedly, the most far-sighted had bread rolls, but they did not share them with the others, hoping that hunger would affect their way with words."

"But Kay, little Kay?" Gerda asked. "When did he arrive? Was he with the others?"

"Give me time, give me time! We are now coming to him. It was on the third day of the event when a little person arrived without a horse or carriage, who walked cheekily towards the castle. His eyes were shining like yours and he had beautiful long hair, but his clothes were like rags."

"It was Kay!" Gerda cried out happily. "Oh, in that case I have found him," and she stood up, clapping her hands.

"He was carrying a bundle on his back," the crow added. "No, it must have been his little sledge," Gerda explained, "because he left home with a sledge."

"It's possible," said the crow. "I did not look closely. My sister told me that when he arrived at the castle gate and saw the guards dressed in silver uniforms and then the valets in gold liveries along the castle staircase, he was not at all embarrassed: instead he waved and said: 'It must be annoying standing there on the stairs, I prefer to go on in.' The rooms were resplendent in the

light of the candles; the counselors and the ministers went about their business in slippers of velvet, interwoven with gold. I am telling you this to make you understand that most people would be embarrassed by the situation! The boy's boots were creaking terribly but he was not embarrassed at all!"

"It's definitely Kay!" Gerda said. "I know that he was wearing his new boots when he left, I heard them creak terribly on the road as he walked away."

"Oh, yes, they were creaking terribly!" the crow confirmed. "But he was walking calmly towards the princess who was sitting on a pearl as large as the wheel of a carriage. All the ladies of the court with the chambermaids, and the chambermaids of the chambermaids, and all the knights with their servants, and the servants of their servants, were standing stock-still around her, and the closer they were to the door, the haughtier they looked. The page of the servants' servant, who always walks barefoot, could hardly be recognized, so proudly did he stand close to the door!"

"That must be horrible!" little Gerda cried out. "And Kay? Did he marry the princess?"

"If I had not been a crow, I would have married her, even if I had already been engaged. He must have spoken very well, as well as I speak the language of the crows: this is what my sister told me. He was brave and gracious. He had not come to ask for the

princess's hand in marriage, but only to find out more about her intelligence that he had heard spoken about, and indeed he found her exceptional, as she found him exceptional."

"That is definitely Kay!" Gerda said. "He was so intelligent: he could do mental arithmetic with fractions! Oh, can you not help me get into the castle?"

"Right, that is easy to say!" the crow muttered. "But how can we do this? I must talk to my sister. She will be able to tell us what to do because, this I must tell you, a little girl like you would never get official permission to enter the castle."

"I am sure I shall get it," Gerda replied confidently. "When Kay knows that I am here, he is sure to come and get me."

"Wait for me there near that passage!" said the bird, then he opened his wings and flew away. He returned when it was already dark.

"Caw, caw, caw!" he said. "I bring you my sister's greetings. And here is a roll for you. I took it from the kitchen, there were so many and I am sure you must be hungry. It is not possible for you to enter the castle: you are barefooted and the guards in silver uniforms and the valets in gold liveries would never allow you in. But do not cry, you will get in all the same. My sister knows a little entrance at the back that leads to the bedroom. She will know where to find the keys." They entered the garden

and walked through the tree-lined avenue, over a blanket of the leaves that had fallen from the branches one after the other. And when all the lights in the castle went out one by one, the crow took little Gerda to a door at the back, which was open. Gerda' s heart was beating wildly with fear and anticipation! She felt strangely guilty at entering the castle surreptitiously, but she relaxed when she remembered that after all she only wanted to find little Kay. It had to be him! Gerda remembered his intelligent eyes and his long hair: she felt as if she could see him smiling in front of her, as he had when they were at home, under the roses. He would certainly be happy to see her and to hear about the long and difficult journey she had made to find him, and how everyone back home was so sad, fearing that he was dead. Oh, it was fear and joy at the same time! Now they were going up the stairs; a little lamp had been lit on a cabinet. In the middle of the floor, the tame crow was waiting for her while constantly looking around, and she watched Gerda curtsey as her grandmother had taught her. "My brother has spoken so well of you, my little lady!" said the tame crow. "You story is very moving! If you take the lantern, I shall lead the way. We will go through this wing of the palace because that way we shall not meet anyone."

"I have a feeling we are being followed," said Gerda. Something made a rushing noise next to her: it was as if there were shadows

on the walls, horses with slender legs, their manes blowing in the wind, young huntsmen, ladies and gentlemen in carriages.

"They are only dreams," said the crow. "At night the thoughts of Their Majesties accompany you hunting and in the park. It is a good thing: in this way you will have a better view of the sovereigns asleep in their beds. I hope that if, thanks to me, you should obtain honors and recognition, you will have a grateful heart."

When they entered the first drawing room, lined with pink satin with a floral motif, the dreams went rushing by, but they passed so quickly that Gerda did not manage to see Their Majesties.

Each drawing room was more beautiful than the last, bewilderingly so! The crow and the little girl moved quietly forward until they reached the bedroom. The ceiling of the room resembled a large palm tree with leaves made of glass, while in the middle of the floor, hanging from a large stem of gold, were two beds, looking like lilies. One was white and that was where the princess slept; the other was red, and that was where Gerda went to look for little Kay. She lifted one of the red petals and saw a brown neck: oh, it was definitely Kay! She shouted his name loudly and went closer with the lamp. The dreams on horseback fled from the drawing room and the prince woke up and turned his head... oh, it was not little Kay! Only the back of his neck was like Kay's, but he too was young and beautiful. The princess emerged from the white lily-shaped bed and asked what was going on. At this point little Gerda started to cry and told her story and everything the crows had done for her.

"Oh, you poor little thing!" exclaimed the prince and princess together, and they praised the crows, adding that they were not angry with them. On the contrary, they would receive a reward. "Would you like to fly away free?" the princess asked, "or would you prefer a well-defined position as court crows with the right to eat everything that is prepared in the kitchen?" Both crows curtsied and said they would be very happy to accept a fixed role. The prince got out of the bed and invited Gerda to sleep in it; but he could do no more than that. The little girl was completely exhausted and she accepted the offer. After curling up on the soft mattress, she closed her eyes and thought: "How kind the people and the animals are in this kingdom." After a few minutes she was sleeping soundly. All the dreams returned, but the scene they showed had changed: they were dragging a little sledge on which Kay was sitting and waving. Unfortunately, it was only a dream and when Gerda woke up, Kay had disappeared again.

The following day the little girl was given new clothes so that now she was dressed from head to toe in silk and velvet; she was invited to stay in the castle, but instead she asked for a small coach and a horse and some little boots so that she could resume her journey throughout the world in search of Kay. She was given boots and a muff: she looked very pretty dressed in them and, just as she was about to leave the castle, another coach stopped in front of the door. It was made of pure gold and displayed the coat of arms of the prince and princess, shining like a star.

The postillion, the servants and the valets on horseback were wearing gold crowns on their heads. The prince and princess helped Gerda climb into the carriage and wished her good luck. The crow from the woods followed her for the first three miles while his sister stayed at the gate and beat her wings: she did not even think of flying because she had been suffering from headaches every since she had taken this permanent job, because she was always able to eat too much. In the coach there were sweet biscuits, and fruit and gingerbread had been put on the seat.

"Farewell! Farewell!" the prince and princess shouted, and when the bird said goodbye, crying, little Gerda too burst into tears. The crow flew away and went to sit on a tree, beating its black wings as a farewell until he could no longer see the carriage, sparkling in the distance as it glistened in the rays of the sun.

All this glitter enthralled the brigands who lived in the dark, impenetrable forest along the road. "It's gold, it's gold," shouted the robbers, running through the wood; they finally reached the highway and cut off the road in front of the carriage. In a few minutes of screams and confusion, the brigands snatched the horses, took the postillion, valets and servants prisoner and dragged little Gerda out of the carriage.

"She is pretty and well dressed," said the old, ugly wife of one of the brigands, pulling a rusty knife from her belt. "She must be a noblewoman, a lady of the court, come here and let me get you ready for the feast... ouch!" She had been bitten in the ear by her little daughter, who had climbed on her back.

"Little brat!" the woman cried.

"Leave that princess alone!" the wild-looking girl shouted in the woman's ear.

"She must play with me! She must give me her muff and her beautiful clothes," and so saying she bit her mother's ear again. Her mother jumped in the air and turned round while all the brigands laughed, saying: "Look how she dances with her daughter!"

"I want to go in the carriage!" said the brigand's daughter, and she managed to get what she wanted because she was very obstinate and spoilt.

She and Gerda climbed into the carriage and carried on over dry scrubland and bushes until they were deep in the wood.

The girl was the same height as Gerda but much stronger and sturdier with a dark skin, and her eyes were so black that they looked like dark wells.

She grabbed Gerda by the waist and said: "They will not kill you if I don't get angry with you! Would you be a princess by any chance?"

"No," the little girl replied, and she told her all about her adventurous journey and how fond she was of little Kay. The brigand's daughter looked at her very seriously, nodded her head and said: "They will not kill you, even if I get angry, because I'll do it myself!" She dried Gerda' s eyes and put her hands in the beautiful muff of soft fur that felt so warm.

The carriage stopped in the middle of the courtyard of the brigands' castle: from top to bottom everything was decrepit, crows and rooks were flying in and out of all the holes in the walls, and enormous mastiffs, big enough to eat a man, were jumping to right and left, but not barking, because that was forbidden.

In the centre of the large, old hall, blackened by smoke, was a big fire over which soup was cooking in a large cauldron while rabbits and hares were turning on a spit.

"You will sleep with me tonight and with all my little animals!" said the brigand's daughter.

They ate and drank, then they went to a corner where they found straw and blankets. A little higher up, on perches and laths, almost a hundreds doves were roosting: they looked as if they were asleep but they moved a little when the girls arrived. "They are all mine," said the brigand's daughter, and quickly she grabbed one of the nearest ones, holding it by its legs and shaking it so that it beat its wings. "Kiss it!" she shouted, pushing it in Gerda's face. "Those are my pigeons!" she continued, pointing at the bars that closed off an opening in the wall. "Those two are wild pigeons. They would fly away if they were not locked up. And here is my beloved reindeer," she added, tugging at the antlers of a reindeer who was tied to the wall with a gold ring through his nose. "He too must remain tied up, or he would run away.

Every evening I scratch his neck with my sharp knife to frighten him!" And having said these cruel words she took a long knife from a crack in the wall and ran it over the reindeer's neck. The poor animal started to kick and the brigand's daughter burst out laughing, then she dragged Gerda with her to bed.

"Do you always keep the knife with you when go to sleep?" asked the girl, who was rather scared at the sight of the weapon.

"Of course! I always sleep with the knife! You never know what might happen. But tell me again what you told me before about little Kay and how you traveled all over the world."

Gerda told her story from the beginning while the pigeons cooed in their cage and the doves slept. The brigand's daughter put her arm round Gerda' s neck, holding the knife in her other hand, and fell asleep. But Gerda was unable to close her eyes, not knowing whether the next day she would be alive or dead.

The brigands were sitting round the fire, singing and drinking, while the brigand's wife was dancing: a horrible, scary sight.

It was at this moment that the pigeons said: "Coo! Coo! We have seen little Kay. A white chicken took his sledge, he was sitting in the carriage of the Snow Queen that was passing through the wood while we were in the nest. It was so windy that all the baby birds died except us two. Coo! Coo!"

"What did you say? Are you sure?" Gerda whispered. "Which

way was the Snow Queen going? Do you know anything?"

"She was certainly going to Lapland because there is always snow and ice there. Try asking the reindeer, who is tied to the wall with the rope," one of the pigeons replied.

"Wherever there is ice and snow, one can be happy there!" the reindeer replied. "One can leap around freely in the wide valleys lit up in the bright moonlight! That is where the Snow Queen's summer camp is, but her castle is near the North Pole on an island called Spitzbergen!"

"Oh, Kay, little Kay!" Gerda sighed.

"Do keep still!" the brigand's daughter muttered, "Otherwise I shall use my knife!"

In the morning Gerda recounted everything the pigeons had said, then, suddenly looking serious, she turned to the reindeer and asked him: "You, tell me, do you know where Lapland is?"

"Who would know better than me?" the reindeer replied, as his eyes lit up with joy, "That is where I was born and grew up, that is where I used to leap across the frozen fields!"

"Listen!" the brigand's daughter said to Gerda. "All the men have gone away, but my mother is still here. When the sun rises she always starts drinking from that large flagon and then she has a little nap: at that moment I shall do something for you!" Meanwhile she jumped out of bed, rushed to her mother, pulled at her

mustache and said: "My darling tramp, good morning!" And her mother pinched her nose until it became red and blue, but these were all signs of affection. When the mother went to have a nap, having emptied the flagon, the brigand's daughter ran to the reindeer and said: "I would very much like to continue scratching you with my sharp knife because you are such fun, but it doesn't matter. I shall cut the rope and help you escape so that you can go back to Lapland. But you must run as fast as possible and take this girl to the Snow Queen's castle where her playmate is. You have heard what she said, because she spoke loudly and you are always listening!" The reindeer jumped for joy and promised to do what was asked. The brigand's daughter helped Gerda climb onto the reindeer's back, tied her tightly to make her safe and even gave her a cushion to sit on. "And here are your fur boots," she cried out, "because it will be cold, but I am keeping the muff because it is so pretty! But to make sure you don't freeze, here are my mother's gloves, they'll probably reach your elbow, put them on."

Gerda cried with joy and gratitude. "I don't like it that you are crying!" the girl said. "You should be happy!" She loaded the provisions onto the reindeer's back, opened the door, locked up all the dogs and cut the rope with the knife, telling the animal: "Run along, go! But take care of the girl." Gerda put on the gloves and leaned down towards the brigand's daughter; she embraced her and said farewell, then the reindeer set off at full gallop, across shrubs and scrubs, through the forest, then across steppes and marshland, as fast as he could. The wolves howled and the crows screeched. Suddenly there was a crackling in the sky: it lit up and turned completely red.

"There are my beloved northern lights!" the reindeer said. "See how they sparkle!" and he ran even faster, day and night, without

getting tired, so happy was he to be free again. And so they soon arrived in Lapland.

They stopped close to miserable-looking hovel: the roof extended down to the ground and the door was so low that the family had to crawl to get in. There was no one at home except for an old lady from Lapland who was frying some fish on a whale-oil lamp. The reindeer told her the story of Gerda, who was unable to speak because she was so cold.

"Oh, you poor things!" the old lady said, "you still have a long journey ahead of you, probably over a hundred miles to get to Finland, because the Snow Queen is holidaying there. We know this because every night the sky is illuminated by large blue fires. I shall write a message on a piece of salt cod, because I have no paper. You must take it to the lady of Finland whom you will find up there: she will be able to give you more detailed information."

So, when Gerda had warmed up, eaten and quenched her thirst, the Lapland woman wrote two lines on a piece of salt cod and told Gerda not to lose it; then she tied the girl onto the reindeer again and said farewell.

The sound "Fut! Fut! Fut!" could be heard in the air and the northern lights shone throughout the night, lighting up the road until they got to their destination.

At last they arrived and knocked on the door of the Finland wom-

an. Inside her house it was so warm that the lady was going about almost without clothing. She immediately helped little Gerda take off her jacket, gloves and boots so as not to be too hot in the red-hot sauna, then she put a piece of ice on the reindeer's head and finally she read what was written of the piece of salt cod.

She read it three times so as to remember it, then threw the fish into the cauldron, because it could be eaten and she never wasted anything; then she asked them to tell her their stories and she listened right to the end without saying a word.

"You are so intelligent", the reindeer said, "I know that you are able to tie together all the winds in the world with sewing thread, so that when the sailor unties one knot, he gets a good wind, if he unties another, the wind will be stronger; if he chooses a third and a fourth, then the wind becomes a thunderstorm and trees will be uprooted. Could you give this little girl a potion that would give her the strength of twelve men so she would be able to defeat the Snow Queen?"

"The strength of twelve men!" the Finland woman said, laughing. "What good would that do?" Then she went to a shelf and took a large piece of rolled-up hide and unrolled it: it was covered in strange letters and she studied it until sweat was pouring down her forehead. But the reindeer asked her again to help the young girl and Gerda herself turned to the Finland woman and looked at

her so imploringly and tearfully that the lady decided she would help her. She took the reindeer into a corner where she whispered something in his ear while putting fresh ice on his head: "Little Kay is indeed with the Snow Queen where he finds everything to his liking, and he believes that this is the most beautiful part of the world. He thinks like this because a piece of mirror got into his heart and another into his eye. First the fragments of mirror must be removed, otherwise Kay will never grow up and he will remain under the Snow Queen's spell."

"But can't you give little Gerda something, a potion or an amulet, so that she would have power over everything?"

"I cannot give her a greater power than she already has! Can't you see how enormous her power is? Don't you see how people and animals serve her and how she has traveled all over the world relying only on her own two legs? She does not need any more power from us than what she already has in her heart, because she is a sweet and innocent young girl. If she does not manage to reach the Snow Queen and remove the fragment of glass from little Kay' s heart, no one will, and we cannot help her! The Snow Queen's garden is about two miles away from here; you must take the girl there and leave her near a large bush with red berries that is there in the snow. But do not hang around there chatting: you must hasten back here at once!" As she was saying this she

helped Gerda climb onto the reindeer, who started running as fast as possible.

"Oh, I didn't bring my boots! Or my gloves either!" shouted little Gerda, who was only now beginning to feel the cold, but the reindeer dared not stop and ran until they arrived at the large bush with red berries. He helped the girl dismount and kissed her on the forehead as big tears ran down his face, then he ran away as fast as he could.

Poor Gerda found herself without a scarf and without gloves in the middle of the terrible freezing country of Finland. She continued running as fast as possible, until suddenly she saw on the horizon a whole army of snow flakes that were not falling from the sky, which was clear and calm. The flakes were running through the middle of the garden and the nearer they got, the bigger they became. Gerda well remembered how large and wonderful they had looked that time when she had seen them through the magnifying glass, but now they were enormous and terrible, alive and frightening. They were the vanguard of the Snow Queen, her carefully selected guards. The closer they got the more Gerda could see that they had the strangest shapes: some looked like horrible fat porcupines, others looked like coiled up snakes with their heads erect, and others again looked like little fat bears with bristly fur, but they were all a dazzling white.

Little Gerda flinched as she recited a prayer and the cold was so strong that she could see her breath in front of her: at first it looked like smoke, then it became denser and turned into little transparent angels who grew larger as they touched the ground. They had helmets on their heads and swords and shields at their sides; they became ever more numerous, and when the little girl had finished praying, there was a whole legion surrounding her. With their swords they struck the horrible snowflakes until they had broken them into a thousand pieces, so that Gerda could move forward safely and confidently. The angels touched her feet and hands: in this way she felt the cold less as they approached the Snow Queen's castle.

But let us first see how Kay was doing.

In all the long months that had passed since he had started following the queen, he had never thought about little Gerda, not even once: the memory of his friend had been driven from his mind and from his heart by the Snow Queen's kiss, and if he had ever known how far his friend had come to find him, he would not have been interested. At this moment, he was quite unaware that Gerda had reached the great doors and passed through them, entering the Snow Queen's castle at last.

The little girl had anxiously crossed the threshold, then, once inside, she looked up and the surprise of what she saw took her breath away: the walls of the palace were made of the snow that fell, while the windows and doors were formed by the winds that blew. In front of her was an impressive staircase, the steps of which were carved out of frozen ice, leading to the first floor, where there were more than a hundred rooms, their sizes changing according to where the snow fell: the largest was many miles long! They were all lit by the northern lights and they were vast, empty, icy and shining bright.

Here there never had been happiness.

Never was there a ball with polar bears dancing, never was there an invitation to dinner for the white lady foxes, everything was empty, enormous and frozen in the rooms of the Snow Queen.

Right in the middle of the last room, which Gerda reached after going along a large corridor at the highest level, she found a frozen lake. It was broken into a thousand pieces, but each piece was identical to the next and it was a real work of art. In the middle of the lake was the Snow Queen's throne and little Kay sat there every day. The child's face and hands were purple, almost black, with the cold, but he did not realize this because with a kiss the Snow Queen had removed his ability to suffer from the cold and had made his heart as hard as a cube of ice.

When Gerda saw him at last, Kay was sitting at the feet of the throne: he was moving some smooth, pointed pieces around,

combining them in all possible ways, because he wanted to make something, rather like when we have some little pieces of wood and put them together to make shapes.

Kay was making various shapes that in his eyes were wonderful and very important, and this was because of the little piece of glass that was in his eye! Then he tried to arrange the letters into words, but when he tried to write "eternity", he could never do it. The Snow Queen had said to him: "If you manage to compose this word, you will be master of yourself and I will give you the whole world and a new pair of shoes." But he was not able to solve the problem: every time he tried, the fragments of ice slid about and moved away from each other, as if controlled by a will of their own.

"I have to leave," the Snow Queen said to him. "I must go to the warm countries to check my black cauldrons." This was the name she gave to the strangest mountains where winter extended in her domain: volcanoes. "I must whiten them a little! Now is the time to do that. And the snow will look very good on the lemons and vines!"

So the Snow Queen flew away, leaving Kay alone in his enormous, icy vaulted rooms to look after his pieces of ice, continuing to concentrate until his head almost exploded, rigid and motionless as if frozen to death.

It was at that moment that little Gerda recognized Kay and ran towards him. When she reached him she threw her arms round his neck, embraced him tightly and cried:

"KAY! SWEET LITTLE KAY! I HAVE FOUND YOU AT LAST!"

But he remained motionless, rigid and frozen. Little Gerda now wept warm tears, which fell on his chest, entered his heart, and melted the piece of mirror that was inside it. Kay looked at her, then burst into tears. He cried so much that the piece of glass fell from his eye, then he rejoiced: "Gerda, sweet little Gerda! Where have you been all this time? And where have I been?" He asked, looking around, terrified. "How cold it is here! How huge and empty everything is!" He hugged Gerda and squeezed her tightly, while she laughed and wept with joy.

It was such a beautiful scene that even the pieces of ice began to dance delightedly around them, and when they were exhausted they stopped, and put the letters in order that the Snow Queen had given Kay to arrange so as to become ruler of himself and to win all the world for himself and a new pair of shoes.

Gerda kissed his cheeks that colored again, then she kissed his eyes that shone like hers, then she kissed his hands and he laughed with all his heart. The Snow Queen might as well go home: the letter of farewell had already been written there, at the foot of her throne, with the pieces of glistening ice. The two children held each other' s hands and left the great castle, talking incessantly about their grandmother and the roses on the roof and where they walked when the winds subsided and the sun shone.

When they reached the bush with the red berries, they found the reindeer waiting for them, with another reindeer, his partner. The two animals accompanied Kay and Gerda first to the Finland woman, where they warmed up in her hot room and asked the way home, then to the Lapland woman, who had sewn them new dresses and gave them a sledge. The two reindeer then began running alongside her and they asked to accompany her to the end of the land, where the first grass was beginning to grow and where the children said farewell to them. "Goodbye!" said everyone.

The children walked along the path and entered the wood. Then from behind a large oak tree a young girl emerged, riding one of the magnificent horses that had pulled the gold carriage. She had a lovely red hat on her head and held a pistol in each hand: it was the brigand's daughter who, tired of being at home, wanted first to go to the North and then to explore other parts of the world. She recognized the little girl immediately and Gerda recognized her, and they were both absolutely delighted to see each other! "You are such a nice person to go round the world!" said Kay. "I would like to know if you deserve people to go to the end of the world for you!" But Gerda patted his cheek and asked about the prince and the princess. "They left for a foreign land," the brigand's daughter replied. "And the crow?" asked Gerda. "Ah, the crow is dead! His sister goes around with a piece of black thread round her leg, mourning him piously, but these are all stories! Now tell me instead what you have been up to." The two children described what had happened to them together and when they had finished the brigand's daughter embraced them and promised that if one day she was passing through their country she would come and see them, then she set off to explore the great wide world. Kay and Gerda walked on hand in hand. Wherever they walked, spring broke out with flowers and greenery and they went on their way laughing together until they saw the tall towers of the great city. This was where they lived: they entered it and walked to the door of their grandmother's house, then they went up the stairs and into the room where everything was just as it had always been, but when they opened the door they realized they had become adults. The roses that were on the gutter were flowering and coming in through the open window.

The children's two little seats were still there: Kay and Gerda sat on them and held hands. Forgotten like a bad dream, they no longer remembered anything about the cold, empty splendor of the Snow Queen's palace. They sat there, both now adults but still children at heart, while the hot summer began at last.